Dear Reader,

I just wanted to tell y
my publisher has decid
earlier books. Some of them have not been available for a while, and amongst them there are titles that have often been requested.

I can't remember a time when I haven't written, although it was not until my daughter was born that I felt confident enough to attempt to get anything published. With my husband's encouragement, my first book was accepted, and since then there have been over 130 more.

Not that the thrill of having a book published gets any less. I still feel the same excitement when a new manuscript is accepted. But it's you, my readers, to whom I owe so much. Your support—and particularly your letters—give me so much pleasure.

I hope you enjoy this collection of some of my favourite novels.

Anne Mather

Back by Popular Demand

With a phenomenal one hundred and thirty books published by Mills & Boon, Anne Mather is one of the world's most popular romance authors. Mills & Boon are proud to bring back many of these highly sought-after novels in a special collector's edition.

ANNE MATHER: COLLECTOR'S EDITION

1 JAKE HOWARD'S WIFE
2 SCORPIONS' DANCE
3 CHARADE IN WINTER
4 A FEVER IN THE BLOOD
5 WILD ENCHANTRESS
6 SPIRIT OF ATLANTIS
7 LOREN'S BABY
8 DEVIL IN VELVET
9 LIVING WITH ADAM
10 SANDSTORM
11 A HAUNTING COMPULSION
12 IMAGES OF LOVE
13 FALLEN ANGEL
14 TRIAL OF INNOCENCE
15 THE MEDICI LOVER
16 THE JUDAS TRAP
17 PALE ORCHID
18 CAROLINE
19 THE SHROUDED WEB
20 A TRIAL MARRIAGE

CHARADE IN WINTER

BY

ANNE MATHER

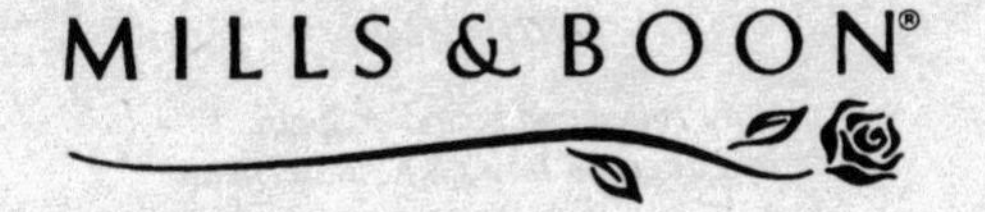

All the characters in this book have no existence outside the imagination of the author, and have no relation whatsoever to anyone bearing the same name or names. They are not even distantly inspired by any individual known or unknown to the author, and all the incidents are pure invention.

First published in Great Britain 1977 by Mills & Boon Limited
This edition 1997
Harlequin Mills & Boon Limited,
Eton House, 18-24 Paradise Road, Richmond, Surrey TW9 1SR

ISBN 0 263 80552 2

Set in Times Roman 10 on 12 pt by
Rowland Phototypesetting Limited
Bury St Edmunds, Suffolk

74-9710-51349

Printed and bound in Spain
by Litografía Rosés S.A., Barcelona

CHAPTER ONE

IT was cold. Much colder than she had expected it would be, even though she had been warned that Northumberland in November was not the place for hothouse plants—Lady Morgan's words, not hers. Her breath turned to vapour in the frosty air, a minute contribution to the mist that was thickening between the trees all around her, giving their bare branches a skeletal shrouding. Alix dug her hands more deeply into the pockets of her sheepskin coat as the tail-lights of the bus disappeared into the encroaching dusk of the afternoon, and then turned reluctantly to the glimmer of light issuing between the half-drawn curtains of the lodge. Had she been mad to agree to this charade? she wondered uneasily. Was she going to regret her impulsiveness before she had even encountered her prospective employer? Was the chill of the day seeping into her bones, undermining her determination to succeed? Or was it simply that she doubted her own ability to cope in what was, to her, an entirely alien situation?

Although there could not be too many buses stopping at the gates of Darkwater Hall, her arrival seemed to have aroused no curiosity, and she looked down resignedly at her two suitcases. As no one else was there to carry them for her, she would have to carry them herself. But how far? The lodge stood just inside the tall iron gates that were at present closed against any intruders, but beyond a curve of gravelled drive that disappeared between thickly planted trees into the mist she could see nothing.

Deciding it was pointless to stand there speculating when action was obviously necessary, Alix looped her handbag over her shoulder and, taking a case in each hand, walked towards the tall gates. An iron ring suspended by the stone gateposts invited tugging, and with an irrepressible feeling of stepping back in time she reached for it.

The sudden barking of dogs was startling and seconds later two enormous wolfhounds rounded the corner of the lodge and came charging towards the gates. She stepped back automatically, the brief spell of unreality evaporating before such an aggressive presence. Instead, the animals renewed all her former uncertainties, and had she not had the suitcases to impede her she might well have changed her mind about going on with this. As it was, she stood in frozen immobility, half mesmerised by the beasts leaping at the gates in front of her, until a man appeared and silenced their noisy uproar. He was an elderly man, dressed in dark trousers and a tweed jacket with leather patches at the elbows, a peaked cap concealing his thatch of silvery hair. He looked neither pleased nor surprised to see her, and without further ado began to unbolt the gates.

'This is Darkwater Hall, isn't it?'

Alix felt obliged to say something, and the man nodded, holding back the dogs by their collars, and indicated that she should come inside. Rather gingerly Alix obeyed, wondering rather foolishly whether he intended letting the dogs loose on her as soon as the gates were closed again.

The gate swung closed behind her, and the man spoke for the first time, his accent thick with the Northumbrian brogue: 'You afraid of dogs?'

Alix put down her cases. 'Not particularly,' she admitted, and then stiffened as he did as she had feared and released the wolfhounds. They came bounding towards her, barking once more, but the man seemed unconcerned.

'They'll not harm you,' he said, securing the gates again, 'not unless you was to run or do something silly like. They're guard dogs, but they're not vicious.'

Alix managed a half-smile, suppressing the urge to push the wet noses away from her legs. 'You know who I am?'

The man regarded her levelly. 'Well, as we don't get young women coming to the gates with suitcases every day, I'd hazard a guess that you was Mrs Thornton, is that right? You're expected. And it's not an afternoon for standing on ceremony, is it?'

'No, it's not.' Alix's pulse rate slowed as the dogs began to lose interest. 'Er—how far is the Hall?'

The man glanced at her, glanced at her suitcases, and then came forward to pick them up. 'Best part of a mile,' he replied laconically, ignoring her dismayed gasp. 'Don't worry, you don't have to walk it. We can go up in the Rover.'

'Thank goodness!' Alix's relief was evident, and the man cast a derisive look at the heels of her boots.

'Them's riding boots, I suppose,' he taunted, and when Alix looked confused, he added, 'Well, they surely don't look like walking boots!' and laughed at his own joke.

Alix didn't find it particularly amusing, but at least his humour helped to relieve the situation, and she managed to ignore the implications behind locked gates and guard dogs and a drive almost a mile in length.

She could see now that a Landrover was parked to one side of the lodge. The lodge itself was a single-storied dwelling, built of local stone, with lead-paned windows and a sloping roof with hanging eaves. It might have been quite picturesque, but in the drifting spirals of mist that crept around it from the forest behind, it, too, had a slightly menacing air.

The Landrover was reassuringly ordinary, and judging from its appearance had spent part of the day ploughing through acres of mud. The man flung her cases into the back with a distinct disregard for their well-being, and Alix felt an almost irresistible urge to rescue them before they, too, became encrusted with mud. But a kind of masochistic desire to go on with this affair kept her still and silent, and she consoled herself with the thought of what an opening to her feature this would make.

The dogs were apparently left loose in the grounds, and when the Landrover's engine was started they slunk away into the shadows surrounding the lodge. The vehicle's headlights made little headway in the mist, but at least they revealed how thickly wooded the area was, and how impossible it must be to see the house from the road. Probably a deliberate choice of landscaping made many years ago when the original inhabitants of the Hall were in residence. Alix had looked up the history of the Darkwaters, thinking that possibly there might be some family connection between old Lord Darkwater and the Morgans: but she could find none. Oliver Morgan's reasons for buying Darkwater Hall and coming to live here were as obscure as ever.

The drive was winding among the trees, and realising she was wasting valuable time, she asked quickly: 'Do you and your wife live at the Lodge, Mr. . .er. . .'

'Giles, ma'am. And I'm not married. Never have been. I manage quite well for myself, and I have the dogs. They're company enough for me.'

'I'm sure they are,' murmured Alix dryly, aware of another pang of discomfort. Were there any other women at Darkwater Hall? And if not, to use a cliché, might she not have bitten off more than she could chew? What did she know of the family that was reassuring? They always made news, but that was more for their notoriety than their popularity, and Joanne Morgan's death in unusual, not to say mysterious, circumstances could not be dismissed. Until now, she had barely stopped to ask herself why Oliver Morgan should require the Darkwater library to be catalogued when he had taken such pains to put himself beyond the reach of would-be sympathisers and press alike. Surely a man in his position would avoid unnecessary visitors in his home—and cataloguing a library, however extensive, could not be an urgent task. But when Willie had first shown her the advertisement, the opportunity it presented had been the most important consideration, and she had not even considered that Lady Morgan could be interviewing some entirely unsuspecting girl on her son-in-law's behalf.

Then she chided herself impatiently. There had been men at the interviews, as well as girls. Oliver Morgan could not have foreseen that the qualifications required might not have been found in a man. He could not have guessed that all but two of the applicants would be deterred by the remote location of Darkwater Hall, or that Alix's magazine would dispose of her final competition by offering the other girl a more lucrative position elsewhere. Besides, this was no time to be getting cold feet. Nothing she had read about Oliver Morgan had led her to believe he was a patient man—as witness his physical ejection of one of her colleagues from an exhibition he had been holding in Kensington, when it had been suggested that without his wife's patronage he might well have found his work harder to sell—and whether or not the exercise was worthwhile she was committed to attempting the job she had been brought here to do. If, in the process, she could discover a little more of the truth behind Joanne Morgan's death and why her husband should now choose to shut himself away in the wilds of Northumbria, so much the better. This was one story no one else should deprive her of, ungrammatical though that might be.

Her only real regret was that she had had to use her mother's name, without her knowledge, to get the references she needed, but when she read the feature her daughter intended to produce, surely she would understand. And if there was no story. . . Alix lifted her slim shoulders in a gesture of dismissal. It shouldn't be too difficult to get herself fired, should it? Although even she had had no idea of the circumstances of her employment, and she doubted anyone could get away—she hesitated over the word escape—from Darkwater Hall without its master's permission.

As Giles seemed disinclined to indulge in casual conversation, the remainder of the journey was accomplished in silence, a silence unbroken by the calls of birds or the sounds of darting insects. The ominous deepening of the mist increased their isolation and aroused in Alix a tension she had never before experienced. With it came thoughts hitherto suppressed—what if Oliver Morgan had had her investigated? What if he had already discovered she was not who she claimed to be? Would he have allowed her to come here in those circumstances? Surely not. Surely if he had even suspected she was a member of the profession he clearly abominated, he would have refused her admission at the gates. Unless he had his own methods for dealing with recalcitrant journalists. . .

But what? She sighed. This was ridiculous! She had always had a vivid imagination and now she was allowing it free rein. And in what direction? It wasn't as if she hadn't seen pictures of Oliver Morgan, she had. She knew what he looked like. Tall and dark, with those hard, intelligent features that older women seemed to go for. Of course, he was quite old—

forty-one or two, but in no way did he resemble the devil, with horns and a tail. And besides, what could he do to her? Her editor knew where she was. The bus driver, and he had certainly paid her enough attention, would surely remember dropping her at the gates of the Hall. And now there was Giles. . .

Alix cast a sideways look at him. Of course, he could be discounted. No doubt he was loyal to his master, and might be prepared to overlook her disappearance. And after all, Joanne Morgan had died in curious circumstances. . .

'Here we are, ma'am.'

Alix started violently. 'What? Oh—yes.' She licked her lips. 'That—didn't take long.'

'No, ma'am?' Giles looked surprised. 'I got the impression you were getting bored.'

'Bored?' Alix almost laughed out loud. 'Oh, no, I wasn't bored.'

Giles contented himself with a wry grimace, and thrusting open his door, descended from the vehicle. For a moment Alix remained where she was, peering through the mud-spattered windows at the house. Wreathed in mist, like the lodge, there wasn't a lot to see, but its stone walls were creeper-clad and solid, the bays on either side of the iron-studded door tall and narrow-paned. Curtains had already been drawn against the darkening day, but the light beyond was heartening.

Giles appeared at her side of the Landrover, and swung open the door. 'Will you come with me?' he requested, and gathering herself with more haste than enthusiasm, Alix obeyed.

She shivered as they mounted the steps to the door, but before Giles could reach the iron bell-rope, the door was opened, and a stream of light dispersed the gloom. An elderly man stood within its illumination, grey-haired and slightly stooped, yet with a not unkindly face.

'Come in, come in, Mrs Thornton,' he urged, when Alix hesitated, waiting for Giles to introduce them then added as she stepped over the threshold: 'I heard the engine coming along the drive, and I guessed you'd be feeling the cold here after London.'

'Thank you.'

Alix stood aside as Giles deposited her cases on the polished floor of the entrance hall, briefly savouring the warmth within, and then felt another wave of anxiety engulf her as, after a tacit farewell, the heavy door was closed, trapping her inside the house. *Trapping!* She quelled the sudden rush of panic. She must stop feeling as if every step she took brought her nearer to Nemesis.

She looked swiftly round the hall, professionally noting the comforting wealth of her surroundings. Panelled walls, gleaming with the patina of age, a fan-shaped staircase, carpeted in green and gold, that forked into two at the first landing and circled the floor above with a carved gallery, a crystal chandelier that cast its light in a thousand trembling prisms. Even the chest that supported a bowl of red and bronze chrysanthemums was inlaid with lacquered panels, and mocked the striking contemporism of the telephone, which seemed strangely out of place. Nevertheless, to Alix, it was a link with the outside world, and therefore more than welcome.

'Did you have a good journey?'

The butler, if he could be termed as such, was speaking, and Alix looked at him with more assurance. 'Yes, thank you. But it's a terrible afternoon.'

The butler nodded. 'The mist—yes, I know. We get a lot of it at this time of the year. It's the dampness, you see, rising among the trees. There are so many trees. . .'

'Not that many. Are you trying to frighten the lady, Seth?'

A film of perspiration broke out on Alix's forehead. She had been so intent on behaving normally that she had been unaware of a door opening across the hall and of the man standing in the aperture, watching them with sardonic amusement. But his words echoed so closely her own imaginary fears that for a minute she was convinced he had called the butler *Death*. She turned so pale that the man shook his head and moved forward in reluctant apology, regarding her with evident impatience.

'I'm sorry if I startled you,' he drawled, and even in her distraught state she noticed how attractive his voice was—deep and husky, almost as though he had a cold, but without the nasal overtones. He looked older than his pictures, as she had expected, and yet he still had the power to disturb her, and she had not expected that. 'What's the matter?' he continued. 'Has our weather convinced you we must have some nefarious purpose for living in such a God-forsaken spot?'

His perception was so acute that her unwilling

admiration brought a little colour back into her cheeks, and his heavy lids shadowed eyes cooling to steel grey. 'So,' he commented dryly, 'I was right. The lady has imagination, Seth. We must see we don't stimulate it more than we can help.'

'No, sir.' The old man bent to lift Alix's cases. 'Shall I show Mrs Thornton to her room, sir?'

Oliver Morgan's dark brows ascended. 'Is that her name?' He paused, and the cold appraisal he gave Alix would not have disgraced a dealer at a cattle auction. 'We haven't yet been introduced, have we?'

His behaviour brought Alix a measure of defensive composure, and holding up her head, she replied sharply: 'Your staff don't appear to consider introductions necessary, Mr Morgan. It is Mr Morgan, isn't it? Not another of his employees!'

His lips twisted in wry acknowledgment of her audacity. 'Yes, I'm Oliver Morgan, although I beg leave to doubt your uncertainty in the matter. However. . .' he indicated the open door behind him, 'I suggest we consider the proprieties satisfied, and continue our discussion in the library.'

Alix looked down at her sheepskin coat, and guessing her thoughts, Morgan added briefly: 'Leave your jacket with Seth. He'll see that your things are taken up to your room while I offer you a drink to dispel your fears, real or imagined.'

The buttons of her coat had never seemed more difficult to unfasten, but at last Seth helped her to shrug out of it and picking up her bag she followed Oliver Morgan into a room lined with books from floor to ceiling. It was a large room, with an iron-runged ladder leading to a narrow gallery which gave access to the books too high on their shelves to be reached by normal methods. The floor was carpeted, there were half a dozen easy chairs, a rather worn-looking table with drawers, and a tapestry-covered sofa faced the hearth, the papers strewn upon it indicating that this was where Oliver Morgan had been sitting. Flames leapt up the chimney from the pile of logs burning in the huge grate, giving the room a comfortable, lived-in air.

Oliver Morgan closed the door behind them, and Alix walked uncertainly towards the fireplace, not quite sure whether she ought to sit down as he did. Still, this was to be her area of activity, and she looked around at the shelves of books with feigned enthusiasm.

Her host had moved to a trolley beside the sofa, and was presently examining the contents of various bottles. Unobserved, Alix attempted to describe him for her own satisfaction, convinced that her initial reactions to him had been merely due to her over-active imagination. In a tweed jacket hardly any less shabby than that of his lodgekeeper, and dark brown cords, his streaked black hair hanging over his collar at the back, he was hardly a figure to quicken her pulse rate, and yet there was an unconscious sensuality about his movements that belied the ill-fitting carelessness of his clothes. She was a tall girl herself, but he was taller, and she guessed that the reason his clothes hung upon him was because he had lost weight. Then he lifted his head, and she felt the same sense of disruption she had experienced in the hall. His own reactions were completely different, however. His features betrayed a certain irritation when he looked at her, and his mouth, with its fuller lower lip, was uncompromisingly straight.

'Whisky or sherry?' he asked now, and guessing he expected her to choose sherry, she chose the opposite. 'Straight?' he queried, pouring a liberal amount of the spirit into a heavy-based glass, and Alix quickly asked for water.

Shrugging, he opened an ice-flask and dropped two cubes into her glass. 'No water,' he said as he handed it to her, and although she was tempted to say something more, she kept silent.

'Sit down,' he said, gesturing towards the easy chairs, and taking him at his word she subsided into the nearest one. He remained standing, which was rather disconcerting, and more disconcerting still was his first comment: 'I have to tell you, Mrs Thornton, you're not exactly what I expected.'

Alix was glad of the glass in her hand. Raised to her lips, it successfully provided a barrier between herself and an immediate reply. But eventually, of course, she had to answer him. 'What—exactly—did you expect, Mr Morgan?'

He had poured himself whisky, too, and this he swallowed straight before speaking again. 'You're younger,' he remarked at last. 'How long have you been married? Doesn't your husband object to you working so far away from London?'

'My—my husband and I are separated,' she responded, giving the reply she had rehearsed.

'Really?' His expression mirrored a certain contempt. 'I wonder why.'

Alix stiffened. 'I don't think that need concern you, Mr Morgan. I'm here to do a job, and providing I do it satisfactorily—'

'Yes, yes, I know.' He cut her off abruptly. 'That still doesn't alter your age—'

'I'm twenty-six, Mr Morgan.'

'Are you?' His eyes narrowed. 'You look younger.'

'I'm sorry.'

He shrugged indifferently. 'I suppose it's of no matter. Presumably Grizelda thought you were suitable.'

'Grizelda?'

'My aunt—my mother-in-law, Lady Morgan. She did interview you, didn't she?'

'Yes.'

'Good.' He turned thoughtfully back to the trolley and poured himself another whisky. 'What did she tell you?'

Alix took another sip of her own drink. Now what was that supposed to mean? What *could* Lady Morgan have told her? Except what qualifications were required for the job.

'I—she told me you wanted someone with a degree in English, and a basic knowledge of at least one other language.' Alix frowned. 'Oh, and some interest in mathematics—for statistical purposes, I suppose.'

He faced her again, feet apart, one hand holding his glass, the other insinuated into the low belt of his pants. 'And that didn't sound unusual to you, did it?'

Alix wished she knew what he meant. 'Not—especially.'

'Tell me, Mrs Thornton, what libraries have you catalogued where such qualifications were necessary?'

Alix trembled. So he *had* had her investigated, after all. He knew she was a fraud, and this was his way of breaking it to her. But how best to deal with it? Ought she to pretend ignorance until he confronted her with her duplicity, or confess her identity forthwith and pray that he wouldn't use physical violence to eject her?

She was still trying to make up her mind, when he went on impatiently: 'You're looking worried again, Mrs Thornton. There is no need, I can assure you. I'm not about to divulge myself as the devil incarnate, nor do I particularly care to take my pleasures with unpaid members of your sex, however delectable they might appear! My dear aunt would not have sent you here otherwise. My questions are purely academic, pertaining to the issues I have to discuss with you. Now—are you reassured?'

Alix was not at all sure she was. But it seemed she had been hasty in assuming he had discovered her identity. 'I—I'm afraid I don't understand you, Mr Morgan,' she ventured demurely, deciding to feign ignorance of the coarser remarks he had addressed to her, and judging from his scornful expression, she had succeeded in this at least.

'Very well.' His nostrils flared. 'I'll come straight

to the point, Mrs Thornton. I did not hire you for a librarian.'

He had succeeded in shocking her now, and Alix came involuntarily to her feet, almost spilling her drink in the process. 'I beg your pardon?'

'You heard me, Mrs Thornton. I did not hire you to catalogue my library.'

Alix's thoughts tumbled wildly. What did he mean? If he did not need to have his library catalogued, why should he go to the trouble of hiring somebody with those qualifications? She stared at him disbelievingly, and he removed his hand from the waistband of his pants to run it carelessly into the open neckline of his dark brown shirt. The movement released another button and the feelings evoked by the curling dark hair escaping through the gap made her realise how vulnerable a woman could be with a man of such unconscious sexuality.

Then he spoke again, and she lifted her eyes to his face. 'For reasons I prefer not to enlarge upon, it was necessary to practise a little subterfuge, Mrs Thornton. My real purpose in bringing you to Darkwater may not be initially to your liking, but I think the remuneration I am prepared to offer will more than compensate you for any inconvenience.'

Alix's fingers felt numb about the glass. 'You said you would get to the point, Mr Morgan,' she said, her voice remarkably even in the circumstances. 'I don't think you have—yet.'

He replaced his empty glass on the trolley, and then put both hands behind his back. 'You're impatient, Mrs Thornton.' He moved to stand before the fire. 'I perceive that's one qualification Grizelda overlooked.'

Alix could feel the tension within herself rising. 'If you don't want a librarian, Mr Morgan, what do you want?' she exclaimed, at a loss to know how her mother would have reacted in this situation, and with a sigh he turned to rest one hand on the mantel.

'A governess, Mrs Thornton,' he said astonishingly, his grey eyes cold and intent. 'I need someone to prepare my daughter for boarding school next September.'

CHAPTER TWO

ALIX's rooms were in the west wing. Carpeted passages led from the first floor gallery into the east and west wings of the Hall, and the overall impression was of great size and grandeur. But in spite of an adequate heating system, Darkwater Hall was too big to feel at home in, and as Alix unpacked her cases and put her belongings away in the capacious cavern of a wardrobe, she couldn't help feeling vaguely anxious. So far as she was aware, she was the only occupant of the west wing, and all those vacant doors she and Seth had passed on the way to her apartments made her feel uneasy.

Not that there was anything to complain about so far as her accommodation was concerned. She had been given adjoining rooms with a private bath, and the sitting room which adjoined this bedroom was extremely comfortable. Most of the furniture was old, but beautifully preserved, and as well as the more traditional items there was a large colour television which would at least help to keep her in touch with the outside world.

The outside world! She shivered. Why was she suddenly thinking of it like that? She was very much of that world, and somehow she would have to maintain contact with it. Willie would be expecting to hear from her, and when he learned why she had been brought here, he would be as astounded as she had been. Oliver and Joanne Morgan had had *no* children. That had been put forward as one of the reasons for the breakdown of the marriage, for long before Joanne died it was known that the relationship between Oliver Morgan and his wife was deteriorating rapidly, and odds were being offered as to when they would eventually split up. But it hadn't happened that way. Joanne Morgan had died instead, arousing a wealth of speculation from every quarter. It was typical of the man himself that he had refused to answer any questions concerning his wife's death, and had left the country three months ago returning, not to London, but to this remote establishment.

No wonder he hadn't wanted to advertise the fact that he required a governess, thought Alix incredulously. This child, whoever she was, was not his wife's offspring, or there would have been no need of the subterfuge he had practised. But apparently the child needed educating, and he was willing to suffer a winter in the north of England if she could be prepared to enter boarding school next autumn. Whether he intended acknowledging her identity at that time, Alix did not care to consider, but her hands trembled when she considered the story this would make. She spread her palms, looking down at their unsteadiness. She must keep calm, she told herself fiercely. On no account must Oliver Morgan learn of her identity, or she hesitated to speculate what his reactions might be.

Fortunately he had taken her startled amazement downstairs to mean what it appeared—the disconcertment of a person hired to do one job who is suddenly faced with another. Anyone would have been shocked to learn they had been hired under false pretences, and indeed, not everyone might have accepted the new arrangements as willingly as she did. Had she been too willing? she asked herself now, and then dismissed the question. It was too late to worry about things like that, when she had so many other matters to worry about, not least her own reactions to the master of Darkwater Hall.

She had never considered herself an emotional person, and her career had always come first with her. The relationships with men she'd had had always remained within the acceptable bounds of affection; and her experiences had never led her to believe that lovemaking was anything more than a rather unnecessary complication she would rather avoid.

Making her plans to come to Darkwater Hall, knowing as she did the reputation Oliver Morgan had acquired, rightly or wrongly, over the years, Alix had never once considered that she might find him attractive. He was too old, for one thing; he was coarse and ill-tempered, and the sensitivity of his work was not reflected in his personal life. Why then did she feel this intense awareness of him as a man, when at no time during their interview had he been anything more than remotely polite with her? He was not handsome, his nose looked as if it had been broken, and the lines drawn so deeply beside his nose and his mouth were pale etchings in his swarthy complexion. And yet something about him sent shivers of anticipation along her spine, and she speedily decided she was mistaking attraction for fear. After all, she had reason to fear him. Nothing could alter that.

With an angry shake of her head, she thrust these disquieting thoughts aside, and marched to the door of the bathroom. She had not met the child yet, but once he had exploded his bombshell, Oliver Morgan had rung for Seth to show her to her room, and suggested she might like to freshen herself before dinner. Perhaps he preferred to give her time to adjust to her new situation before confronting her with her charge. Certainly the turn of events demanded adjustment, even for her, and she understood now why the qualifications had been so unusual. And yet it was not an unimaginative idea. Someone of her mother's abilities would be quite capable of instructing a child to preparatory level, and Alix only hoped she was equally able.

The bathroom was as large as the other apartments, with an enormous sunken bath made of veined green marble. The mixer and taps were shaped in bronze, like a lion's head; the taps the claws, the mixer the beast's yawning jaws. Long mirrors lined the walls above the bath, and panelled the inner side of the heavy door. As Alix shed her clothes, she saw her reflection thrown back at her from a dozen different aspects, and a faint flush of colour stained her cheeks. She had never contemplated her nakedness in such detail, and she was glad when the bath was full of heated soapy water, and the mirrors filmed with steam.

Nevertheless later, as she towelled herself dry with

an enormous fluffy green bathsheet, she found herself wondering what kind of woman would appeal to a man like Oliver Morgan. Not someone like herself, she decided. No doubt he preferred smaller women, some dark delicate creature, with consumptive pallor and blue eyes, similar to the pictures she had seen of his wife. Certainly not a tall, bosomy blonde, who looked well able to take care of herself.

Wrapping herself in a towelling bathrobe she had found behind the door, she went back into her bedroom and seated herself before the dressing table mirror. Her hair was shoulder-length and uncompromisingly straight, and she brushed it vigorously, finding a certain amount of release in the effort it required. Then she applied a mascara brush to her lashes, darkening the gold-flecked tips and outlining the wide spacing of eyes that were an unusual shade of green. Her eyes were her best feature, she had decided long ago, ignoring the generously warm fullness of her mouth.

She wasn't sure whether or not she was expected to dress for dinner, or indeed where she would take her meals. Her knowledge of governesses didn't encompass their eating habits, and the thought of sharing Oliver Morgan's table every evening was a daunting one. During the day, she would no doubt be expected to supervise his daughter's meals, but after she had gone to bed—what then? Other thoughts occurred to her. Were governesses expected to see their charges into bed? Who attended to the child's physical needs, mended her clothes, combed her hair? Alix shook her head. It was as well Oliver

Morgan had employed her as a librarian. At least he would not expect her to be *au fait* with the duties of a governess.

She eventually decided to wear a dress of dark green silk jersey, its midi-length skirt swinging about her hips, the deep vee of the bodice exposing the swell of her full breasts. It was not perhaps the most suitable attire for a governess, but after all, that was not her designation, assumed or otherwise, and she saw no reason to dress down to her position. Besides, the child was probably used to seeing much more extravagantly dressed women, and Alix wondered briefly where she had been brought up, and by whom.

She was giving her hair a final flick with the comb when someone knocked at the door of her sitting room. She glanced at her watch and saw with surprise it was already after seven. Guessing Seth had come to tell her that dinner was ready, she swung open the door, and stared aghast at the tiny figure outside.

Could this be Oliver Morgan's daughter? she wondered fleetingly, and then speedily dismissed the idea. The creature before her, dressed in a lavishly-embroidered kimono, was female certainly, and scarcely above a child's stature, but an infant she was not. The painted face staring up at her was lined and old, the lacquered hair obviously tinted, and slanting almond eyes had receded far into her head. Alix guessed she was Japanese, and wondered in amazement what she was doing in Oliver Morgan's house.

'Mrs Thornton?'

The woman was speaking in a shrill lisping tone,

and Alix nodded her head quickly. 'Yes, I'm—Mrs Thornton. I—can I help you?'

Thin lips curved in the semblance of a smile. 'You have come to take care of my missy?'

Alix's eyes widened. 'Missy? That would be—Miss Morgan?' She moved her head in a confused gesture. 'I believe so. Who are you?'

'My name is Makoto.' The small figure performed an obeisance that came somewhere between a bow and a curtsy. 'Most happy to make your acquaintance, Thornton *san*.'

Alix put out a deprecating hand. 'Oh, please—that is—did you want to see me, Makoto?'

'Missy wishes to meet new governess, Thornton *san*. You will come with me?'

Alix glanced round at the room behind her. Confusion was giving way to curiosity, but she had no idea whether Oliver Morgan would approve of her meeting his daughter without his knowledge.

'You will come, please?'

The old woman was speaking again, and Alix turned back to her ruefully. Obviously Makoto considered her mistress's commands should be obeyed, and if she was anything like her father, then perhaps that wasn't so difficult to understand. All the same, Alix wasn't happy about the situation.

'Er—Mr Morgan is expecting me to join him for dinner—' she began awkwardly, and then gave an exasperated exclamation when Makoto performed another of her low bows and began to walk away. The last thing she wanted right now was hostility between herself and Morgan's daughter, particularly when the situation was turning out to be such an intriguing one. A remote house, a child that no one knew existed—and now a Japanese servant! 'Hey!' she called, impulsively going into the passage and closing her bedroom door. 'Hey, wait! I'll come.'

Makoto's paper-white face expressed her satisfaction. She waited for Alix to catch up with her, and then adjusted her small, half-running steps to Alix's larger strides. If anything had been needed to convince Alix of the disadvantages of her size, walking beside the tiny Japanese woman would have done it, although judging from the admiring glances Makoto kept directing towards her, in her case the opposite could apply.

They crossed the gallery at the head of the stairs, and continued on into the east wing. Alix couldn't resist glancing down into the hall below, half afraid that Oliver Morgan might be standing there watching them, but there was no one about, and she breathed a little more easily.

Makoto halted at the door at the end of the corridor, and turning the handle indicated that Alix should precede her into her room. Alix did so, not without some misgivings, and then came to an abrupt halt at the foot of an enormous tester bed. A child, perhaps eight years old, was sitting up in the bed, almost lost among so many pillows, her dark hair hanging in one thick braid over her shoulder. She was wearing a white nightgown which accentuated the paleness of her skin, for although her features were European, her eyes had a definitely oriental slant. But she was beautiful, even Alix saw that in those first astounded moments, and when she smiled her small teeth were as perfectly formed as the rest of her. Delicately small hands plucked impatiently at the bedcovers, and her whole demeanour was one of suppressed excitement.

So this was Oliver Morgan's secret, thought Alix, feeling curiously shaken by the revelation. This was why the child had been kept out of the public eye, and why he had chosen to bring her back to a house as remote from London as he could find. The child's mother had probably been as Japanese as old Makoto who stood so proudly beside her, her gnarled hands folded into the wide sleeves of her kimono, while his wife had been as European as he was.

'Hello. I'm Melissa.' The child's voice surprisingly bore no Eastern intonation, but was as English as Alix's own. 'Are you Miss Thornton?'

Alex collected herself with difficulty. 'I—I'm *Mrs* Thornton,' she amended reluctantly. 'How do you do, Melissa?'

The little girl beckoned her nearer the bed. 'Are you really married? Do you have any children of your own?'

Alix flicked an embarrassed look in Makoto's direction, but fortunately the Japanese woman was regarding her charge with evident satisfaction. 'No,' she answered uncomfortably, 'I don't have any children.'

Melissa's small shoulders sketched a regretful shrug, and then she went on eagerly: 'Have you come to stay with us? Daddy says you have. He says I have to go to an English school, and learn to be an English lady, and you're going to help me.' she paused. 'Are you an English lady, Mrs Thorn—'

'*Melissa!*'

Oliver Morgan's voice was full of irritation, and Alix turned her head to see the master of the house striding into his daughter's bedroom with evident annoyance. His appearance—he was dressed in black suede pants and a black silk shirt—was sufficiently grim to daunt the most intrepid heart, but Melissa's reactions were totally without fear. Pushing back the covers, she thrust her small legs out of bed, and rushed across the floor to reach him, and with only a half-hearted protest her father swung her up into his arms. But not before Alix had glimpsed the flaw in the perfection—Melissa was lame.

Her eyes lifted to encounter the incisive scrutiny of Oliver Morgan's gaze, and she knew he was waiting for her reactions. But she refused to give him the satisfaction of knowing she had been shocked, about anything, and before the child could launch into her explanations, she said: 'Melissa and I have been getting to know one another.'

'You're not cross, are you, Daddy?'

Melissa's arms were around his neck, modestly hidden beneath wrist-length sleeves, but her leap into his arms had brought the hem of her nightgown up round her thighs and Makoto was trying desperately to pull it down.

Oliver Morgan brushed the Japanese woman away, and looked into his daughter's mischievous face. 'You were supposed to wait until tomorrow morning to meet Mrs Thornton,' he told her, but there was indulgence in his tone, and Alix was amazed at the tenderness in his expression.

'I couldn't wait,' said Melissa simply, his face cupped between her two small palms. Then she flashed a smile at Alix. 'She's not at all like you said she would be, is she?'

'Young ladies do not make personal remarks,' observed her father dryly, allowing her to slide to the floor. 'And now, I suppose, Makoto will have the devil's own job getting you settled down again.'

'Makoto brought Mrs Thornton here,' stated Melissa, reluctant to return to the bed, and Oliver Morgan's eyes turned in Alix's direction, subjecting her to another of those raking appraisals such as he had given her downstairs.

'I guessed that,' he conceded, irritation tightening his lips, as if he blamed Alix for upsetting the child. Then he turned to Makoto, and speaking rapidly in a language Alix couldn't begin to comprehend made his demands known.

'Daddy is telling Makoto that you are here to give me lessons only, not to entertain me,' translated Melissa artlessly, arousing an impatient oath from her father, and Alix decided that the time had come for her to leave. But the child was intriguing, and she was loath to go without reassuring her on that point at least.

'I'm sure we'll have plenty of time to entertain each other,' she told her lightly, as Melissa obeyed her father's terse directions and limped back to the bed.

Alix walked pensively to the head of the stairs,

and then began to descend them slowly. She had reached the central landing when Oliver Morgan caught up with her. He passed her without a glance, however, and then stood waiting at the foot of the stairs, watching her come down the rest of the way with what she was beginning to recognise as his usual taut expression. He made her nervous and in consequence she stumbled, but apart from a further tightening of his lips, he made no acknowledgment of her small accident.

'Would you like a drink before dinner?' he inquired when she had reached the comparative safety of the hall, but she shook her head. In truth, the whisky she had drunk earlier had been stronger than she had imagined, and she needed no further dulling of her wits where Oliver Morgan was concerned.

'Then I suggest we go straight in to dinner,' remarked her host briefly, and led the way across the hall and into the dining room.

Like the other rooms of the house, it was large, but as it was filled with a long polished table, flanked by a dozen tall-backed chairs, a pair of matching sideboards and a huge Welsh dresser, it did not seem excessively so. One end of the table had been set with two places—heavy silver cutlery, Waterford crystal and Crown Derby—and as they entered, a girl came through another door at the far end of the room which probably gave access to the kitchens.

Alix was relieved to see that there was a girl of around her own age at Darkwater Hall, and she looked pointedly at Oliver Morgan, waiting for him to introduce them. He seemed strangely loath to do so, however, although from the avid way the girl was looking at him, she had no objections. In fact there was something faintly repelling about the dog-like devotion in the girl's eyes as she pulled out his chair for him, and the way her mouth gaped when he thanked her. Alix quickly subsided into the vacant seat to his right, and the girl cast a vaguely hostile look in her direction before disappearing again, no doubt in pursuit of the first course.

The room was illuminated from a central chandelier, and the light glowed ruby red in the bottle of wine Oliver lifted to fill her glass. 'You look disapproving, Mrs Thornton,' he said, his eyes mocking hers. 'Myra and her mother, Mrs Brandon, take care of all the cooking and cleaning here.'

Alix's fingers sought the stem of the glass. 'I see.'

'Do I detect disapproval in your tones?' His brows ascended. 'It might not yet have become obvious to you, but Myra—isn't quite as other girls. What I'm trying to say, not very successfully I'm afraid, is that Myra's mental capacity is limited.'

'Oh.' Alix felt chastened.

'You hadn't noticed?'

Alix shrugged. 'Not really. . .'

'You weren't offended by her behaviour?'

'Offended? No.'

'Affronted, perhaps?' His lips curled. 'You have very expressive features, Mrs Thornton. You'll have to learn to control your feelings if you don't want me to know what you're thinking.'

Alix, used as she was to awkward confrontations

in the course of her work, could nevertheless feel a faint deepening of colour at his words. He was altogether too perceptive, and she would have to be on her guard for more reasons than he knew.

In an effort to change the subject, she said: 'How old is Melissa?' and saw the immediate hardening of his profile.

'She's eight,' he replied abruptly, and was saved from continuing by the return of the girl, Myra, with a tureen of soup. 'We can help ourselves Myra,' he told her firmly, after she had set soup plates before them, and she nodded rather sulkily and left them again.

It was leek soup, home-made, Alix guessed, and aromatically delicious. It made her realise that she had eaten nothing since lunchtime, and she needed no second bidding to fill her plate. She accepted a roll from the basket he offered, and began to spoon up the creamy liquid eagerly. It took her a few minutes to realise he had not followed her example, and she looked up to find him watching her with a curious expression on his lean features, his glass of wine held lazily in his hand.

At once she was on the defensive again, and feeling rather like a child in the company of an adult, she put down her spoon and said: 'I'm sorry. I—I was hungry.'

He leaned back in his chair at the end of the long table, looking very much the master of the situation, and she wondered why his eyes upon her made her conscious of every inch of flesh she was displaying. Her hand went automatically to the low neckline of her dress, seeking and finding the medallion that swung there between her breasts, holding on to it as if to a lifeline.

'Please,' he said, without mockery, gesturing with his free hand, 'do go on. I'm sorry if I embarrassed you, but it's quite refreshing to discover that there are women who enjoy their food. My own experience has been limited to the other kind.'

Alix looked down at her plate. 'But you're not eating,' she exclaimed, looking up again.

He shrugged. 'My appetite is not what it was, Mrs Thornton. But please don't let my inadequacy prevent you from enjoying your meal. Mrs Brandon is an excellent cook.'

Unwillingly, Alix picked up her spoon again and continued with the soup. But it was so delicious that after a while she forgot that his eyes might be upon her, and finished every drop.

'Some more?' he suggested, when she looked up, but she shook her head, and was glad when Myra arrived to remove their plates.

The main course was chicken, sliced and cooked in a sauce made with white wine, and served with vegetables on a bed of flaky rice. Alix noticed that although her host helped himself to a little of this, he spent the time it took her to eat her helping pushing his around his plate, and drinking several glasses of a dry white wine he had opened after finishing the red wine practically singlehanded.

When Alix refused a second helping of the delectable raspberry gateau which completed the meal and coffee had been served, Oliver Morgan produced a thick cigar and after gaining her assurance that she had no objections to his lighting it, said: 'Now, Mrs Thornton, I suggest we get the preliminaries over with, and then we can perhaps get down to business.'

'The preliminaries?' Alix frowned. 'I'm sorry, but—what do you mean?'

He rose from his seat to light his cigar, and then regarded her dourly. 'Come, Mrs Thornton, don't be coy. I was hoping to delay your introduction to my daughter until the morning, but I ought to have realised that curiosity would get the better of discretion.'

Alix looked up at him. 'I did not go in search of your daughter, Mr Morgan.'

'I know that,' he retorted shortly, 'but you've seen her now, and I can't believe you haven't noticed that she's partly Japanese.'

'She's a beautiful child,' said Alix honestly.

He frowned. 'How much do you know of my family, Mrs Thornton?'

Alix was taken aback. 'I—I—'

'Oh, come on!' He was impatient. 'You surely must have heard of us before you came here.'

'I know you're a sculptor, Mr Morgan.' Alix tried to limit her thoughts to what any average housewife might know. 'I saw your last exhibition. I thought your interpretation of the Seven Sinners was marv—'

'I'm not looking for compliments, Mrs Thornton, I'm merely trying to ascertain your reactions to my daughter. You're not deterred?'

'Deterred?' Alix was confused now. 'I don't understand.'

His sigh was the only sign of his irritation. 'Mrs Thornton, it is not conceit when I tell you that anything and everything I do is closely monitored by the press. I accept that. You cannot expect to seek the public eye without its being turned upon you—for good or ill. But I regret to say that my own dealings with the press have not been without incident.' He paused, and she made a pretence of examining the coffee in her cup to avoid his eyes. 'In consequence, I am loath to subject the child upstairs to that kind of atmosphere without first preparing the way. You realise now why I couldn't advertise for a governess. My wife and I had no children, as you're probably aware, and Melissa's upbringing has been sheltered until now.'

Alix wondered how he would feel when he learned he had confided these thoughts to a professional journalist, and inwardly shivered. This job was not turning out at all as she had imagined, and she wondered whether she would have been as keen to come here had she known a child was involved. And yet, looking at the situation from Joanne Morgan's point of view, Melissa was merely a further endorsement of the unsavoury character of the man, and if she was to be hurt in all this she had only her father to blame.

Forcing herself to speak objectively, Alix asked: 'Where has Melissa been living?' and witnessed his automatic gesture of withdrawal.

'I could say that need not concern you, Mrs Thornton,' he remarked dryly, 'but knowing Melissa as I do, if I don't tell you, she undoubtedly will. She was born in Tokyo, but she has lived all her life in Hokkaido, the northernmost island of the group.' He studied the glowing tip of his cigar for a moment, and then went on: 'Until quite recently, she was being looked after by an elderly English lady who had made her home in Japan, and that is why Melissa speaks our language so well. But unfortunately, Miss Stanwick died before I could bring them both back to England, and consequently other arrangements had to be made.'

'I understand.'

'I doubt you do, Mrs Thornton,' he contradicted her, 'but perhaps we'll come to understand each other.'

Alix hoped not. 'I'll do what I can,' she said non-committally, and then got to her feet. 'If—if that's all, Mr Morgan, it's been a long day, and I am rather tired—'

His scowl silenced her. 'I'm afraid that's not all, Mrs Thornton. If you've finished your coffee, I suggest we adjourn to the library so that Mrs Brandon can get the table cleared.'

He moved lithely towards the door, and she had perforce to follow him, very conscious of the controlled muscular strength of his body. What chance would she have against that whipcord hardness of flesh and sinew, she asked herself, if ever that explosive temper of his was turned in her direction? There was not an ounce of surplus flesh on him, and whatever kind of life he had been leading, it had not softened him. Willie's description of the man as a temperamental bastard, full of his own importance, was no comfort in this situation.

She refused the liqueur he offered her in the library, and perched on the edge of the chair she had occupied earlier, waiting for him to speak. Eventually he came and took the chair opposite, at the other side of the hearth, sitting with his legs apart, his hands cradling a brandy glass suspended between them.

'I want to explain what I expect of you, Mrs Thornton,' he said at last, and she tried to meet his eyes without flinching. 'You noticed that Melissa is lame, I know that, but she's not stupid. She can read—not well, I admit, but she is literate. However, that is not enough. I want her to read fluently. I want her to understand simple mathematics, and if there's time, perhaps a little general knowledge could be included.' Alix nodded, and he went on: 'Your application also implied that you could speak both French and German. While I appreciate that you're not a teacher, Mrs Thornton, and all this will be new to you, it may be possible to instruct Melissa in a language as well.'

Alix cleared her throat. Her mother, certainly, was fluent in several European languages, but her own abilities were less impressive. 'I—French is my best subject,' she managed, and he seemed to accept that.

'There is the final matter of Makoto,' he added. 'She has cared for the child since she was born, and you may find her presence irritating at times.' He paused. 'She must be made to understand that while Melissa is working, she does not get in the way.'

'I'm sure that can be arranged,' said Alix quickly, and he inclined his head.

'So.' He lay back in his chair, stretching his long legs lazily, and raising the brandy glass to his lips. 'I suggest you use this room for the lessons. I've taken the liberty of obtaining some textbooks, which you might study tomorrow, and the following day perhaps you could begin.' He grimaced into his glass as if it no longer appealed to him, and then sat upright again. 'I'm sorry if you feel I'm behaving like a slavedriver, but I have work to do as well, and I want to get these arrangements done with.'

'That's all right.' Alix moved her shoulders deprecatingly. 'So—so long as you don't expect too much. . .'

'I always expect too much, Mrs Thornton,' he replied with irony. 'That's why my life has been one long disappointment to me.'

Alix got to her feet. 'I—I'll say goodnight, then,' she asserted, not quite knowing how to answer him, and his lips twisted.

'You're not concerned that your reputation might suffer when it's ultimately revealed that you've been living here with me?' he inquired, looking tauntingly up at her, and she realised the amount of alcohol he had consumed throughout the evening was responsible for the slight glazing of his eyes.

'I—no.' She stilled the involuntary movement of her hand towards her throat again. And when he persisted on looking at her, she added: 'I don't think so.'

'Your husband isn't likely to come lusting for my blood?'

'Of course not.' She silently damned the revealing colour that entered her cheeks.

'Good.' With an economy of movement, he was on his feet and facing her, only a stride away. 'I should hate to have to contend with the kind of publicity that would generate.'

'You won't,' she assured him tautly, wishing she was not so conscious of his nearness.

'You must have married out of the schoolroom,' he observed insistently, and she saw his eyes move to the quickening rise and fall of her breasts.

'Not—not quite,' she stammered, feeling exposed, and with an indifferent shrug he moved away from her, leaving her weak and shaken by emotion.

'Goodnight then, Mrs Thornton.' He was opening the door for her, and she passed him with a mumbled salutation, crossing the hall to the stairs on legs which had never felt so uncertain.

She hadn't expected to feel relieved to reach the isolation of her room, but she did. She closed her sitting room door and leaned back against it wearily, aware of feeling more exhausted than circumstances warranted. Then she expelled her breath on a sigh and straightening, walked through the lamplit apartment to her bedroom.

Someone had turned down her bed in her absence, and her nightgown had been draped carefully across the sheet. She wondered whether Myra had done it, and thinking of the other girl reminded her of the way she had looked at Oliver Morgan. However retarded her mental condition, physically she was a woman, and it was as a woman she had looked at her master. But how did he see her? She was not an unattractive girl, and he was a man with the same needs as any other man. And yet he had told Alix that he preferred to pay for his pleasures. Did he pay Myra?

She shuddered at the inclination of her thoughts, and tightening her lips, began to undress. But before she put on her nightgown, she ran her hands down over her breasts, her palms covering the hardening nipples. She felt strangely disturbed by the knowledge that a man like Oliver Morgan could arouse her in this way, and she stared at her reflection with unconcealed dislike. She had never felt this sense of discovery about herself before, and it was galling to find it coming between her and her work.

With a grimace of annoyance she reached for her nightgown, and allowed its filmy folds to fall about her ankles. Then she went into the bathroom to wash and clean her teeth, determinedly putting all thoughts of Oliver Morgan out of her mind. She was tired. Things would look different in the morning.

But once she was in bed, between sheets which she discovered were made of silk, it was not so easy to get to sleep. She had peeped through her curtains before getting into bed, and the mist outside seemed to be pressing against the window panes, imprisoning her in this isolated oasis of civilisation. Last night, sleeping in her own bed in her flat in London, she had had no notion of the complications she would find at Darkwater Hall, and there was something rather frightening in the remoteness of that thought. . .

CHAPTER THREE

THE next morning Alix slept late, which wasn't surprising after she had lain awake for several hours listening to the creaking of the old house as it settled down for the night. Her flat in London overlooked a busy thoroughfare, and the unaccustomed silence here, broken only by contracting boards and soughing trees, was all strange to her. But eventually she had slept, and she awakened feeling refreshed and relaxed.

But the relaxation didn't last long. One look at her watch, which she had left on the table beside the bed, and she was thrusting back the bedclothes, crossing the carpet eagerly to draw back the curtains.

It was after ten o'clock, and a rosy haze was gradually dispersing the shreds of mist that lingered among the sheltering belt of trees. Now that it was light, she could see that her room was at the front of the house, and beyond the sweep of courtyard acres of rolling parkland stretched away in all directions. The grass still shimmered with the heavy dew left by the mist, and there was a clean, drenched freshness about everything that made even the bare branches of the trees project a tracery of beauty. Some of the trees still clung to their leaves, and colours of yellow, bronze and amber mingled with the heavy greens of pine and spruce. It was a world away from the urban surroundings she was used to, and Alix wondered at her own capacity to adapt to it without constraint.

But enchanting though the prospect from her window was, cold reality began to intrude. This was her first day at Darkwater Hall, and she had overslept. Hardly the way to begin, she thought ruefully, going into the bathroom, and turning on the shower. No matter how intriguing her surroundings might be, she was here to do a job, and not just the task Oliver Morgan had set her. Melissa's presence could well turn out to be the key to the whole mystery surrounding Joanne Morgan's death. What if Mrs Morgan had been kept in ignorance of the child's existence, and had suddenly found out? What if she had threatened to expose him? He was a man of uncertain temper, everyone knew that. To what lengths might he have been prepared to go to stop her?

Alix shook her head impatiently, stepping out from under the invigorating spray and towelling herself dry. This was all pure speculation! Joanne Morgan had died as the result of a car crash. It had been an accident. The coroner had recorded a verdict of accidental death. Just because her husband had inherited a vast amount of money from her estate it did not mean he had had a hand in loosening the brakes or the steering wheel, or had crippled the car in some other way so that she wrapped it round a tree only half a mile from their house in Sussex.

Nevertheless, people were talking, and if it was ever revealed that he had had a Japanese mistress tucked away somewhere. . . Alix brought herself up short. What did she mean—*if*? Of course it would be revealed. This was *her* story, the one which would make her famous. She must not let sentimentality for the child undermine her determination. She would stay here just as long as it took to get to know Oliver Morgan, to find out what made him tick, and if possible to hear his version of his wife's accident. Melissa's mother was another story, and some other sensation-minded reporter could dig up those sordid details.

She dressed in slim-fitting orange pants and a shirt in an attractive shade of olive green. Make-up she limited to eye-liner and lipstick, and feeling the familiar pangs of hunger she hurriedly made her bed before making her way downstairs.

A grey-haired, middle-aged woman was working in the hall, polishing the carved chest Alix had admired the previous evening, and she looked up with evident curiosity when Alix came down the stairs.

'Good morning,' she replied in answer to Alix's greeting. 'Mrs Thornton, isn't it?'

Alix's thumb went self-consciously to the plain gold band she could feel on her third finger, but she nodded quickly. 'That's right. You must be Mrs Brandon. I'm sorry I'm so late, I overslept.'

The woman was taller than she had appeared from above, and they were almost on eye-level terms when Alix reached the hall. 'Mr Morgan had breakfast a couple of hours ago,' she added half-accusingly. 'Will you be wanting a meal?'

Alix hesitated. But she couldn't go all morning without food. 'Perhaps some toast—and coffee?' she ventured, and Mrs Brandon sniffed.

'Very well, I'll get it.'

'Oh, please. . .' Alix didn't want to be a nuisance. 'I can look after myself. If you'll show me the way to the kitchen—'

Mrs Brandon shook her head, folding her arms across her flowered overall. 'I said I'd get it, Mrs Thornton. The kitchen is no place for *governesses*!'

The way she said that word made Alix stare at her with troubled eyes. What was wrong with being a governess, for heaven's sake? And in any case, surely Mrs Brandon must know she had been hired as a librarian.

The older woman gave her another contemptuous look, and then walked briskly across the hall to a door set beneath the curve of the staircase. Alix watched her go with misgivings, and then, shrugging her slim shoulders, she glanced round. She recognised the door to the library, with its distinctive leather soundproofing, and the door to the dining room stood wide, but there were several other doors and she decided to explore.

The first room she entered was a drawing room, high-ceilinged and magnificent, with a genuine Adam fireplace and an enormous grand piano. Long couches, upholstered in dusty pink velvet, were standing on a fine cream carpet, the pattern of which was obviously Chinese, and there were tall cabinets flanking the fireplace filled with a collection of ivory and jade.

Alix closed the door again rather reverently, and started guiltily when a hand tugged at her arm. It was Mrs Brandon's daughter Myra, and she was pointing rather angrily towards the dining room.

'You come,' she insisted, half pulling the other girl across the hall, and Alix offered no resistance.

A place had been set for her at the table, and although she would have preferred a tray to take up to her sitting room, she had to admit that Mrs Brandon had gone to a great deal of trouble on her behalf. There was some freshly-squeezed orange juice, warm rolls as well as a rack of toast, a selection of conserves and marmalades on a silver dish, and a jug of steaming aromatic coffee all to herself. Myra saw her into her seat, and then stood looking at her rather unnervingly.

'This is delightful, Myra.' Alix endeavoured to show her appreciation. 'I promise tomorrow morning I'll be down as soon as Mr Morgan.'

The girl hunched her shoulders. 'Morgan—he said you were tired.'

Alix smiled. 'Well, he was right,' she exclaimed, rolling her eyes expressively. 'That was some journey yesterday.'

Myra looked no less hostile. 'You sleep with Morgan?' she demanded aggressively, and Alix dropped the knife she had been using to butter her toast.

'*No!*' she denied hotly, endeavouring to remember that Myra was not quite normal. 'I mean—of course not.'

Myra frowned. 'Morgan brought you here,' she stated, as if that was enough.

Alix sighed. 'To—to teach Melissa. His daughter!'

Myra was obviously trying to absorb this. 'You're

a teacher?' she asked suspiciously, and Alix sighed again. How did she answer that?

'I—yes,' she said at last. 'Yes, I'm a teacher.'

'I thought you was a librarian, Mrs Thornton.'

Unknown to Alix, Mrs Brandon had come through the door from the kitchen, and was standing regarding the two girls with her hands on her hips.

Alix put down her knife again. 'I am. But I was just trying to explain to your daughter—'

'I heard what you was saying to Myra,' retorted Mrs Brandon, repressively, 'and she doesn't have time to stand around gossiping to the likes of you.' Before Alix could protest, she gestured to the girl to get about her business, and then disappeared herself back into the kitchen.

Alix retrieved her knife again, but her appetite had gone. Between them, Mrs Brandon and her daughter had succeeded in making her feel little better than a call-girl brought here in the guise of a librarian to keep their employer happy. She didn't know which of them, Oliver Morgan or herself, it reflected least favourably upon, but she suspected they had no doubts on that score.

She poured a second cup of coffee and stared broodingly at a painting hanging above the sideboard opposite. It depicted a farming scene and could conceivably be a Constable, but it was not the sort of thing she particularly admired. Nevertheless its uncomplicated harmony was soothing, and by the time she had finished her coffee she had herself in control again.

There was still no one about when she emerged

from the dining room, and she wondered where Oliver Morgan could be. Melissa, too, was conspicuous by her absence, for Alix had felt sure she would be eager to meet her new governess again.

She decided to go into the library as that was the place where Oliver Morgan expected her to work, and the cosy fire she found there lifted her spirits. The heavy maroon drapes had been drawn back from the windows to reveal that they overlooked the back of the house, where a stone terrace gave on to lawns and flower-beds, sadly lacking in colour at this time of the year. A few hardy roses still survived against the increasingly frosty air, but almost everything else had given up the struggle.

She turned back to the room and discovered that the textbooks Oliver had spoken of the night before had been laid out on the table awaiting her inspection, and she spent the next hour going through them. She was enjoying the delights of one of the story books Oliver Morgan had also provided when she heard voices outside, and curiosity made her get up and go to the windows again.

Oliver Morgan and his daughter were walking towards the house from the direction of the surrounding belt of trees, laughing and talking together with an easy camaraderie. They were both wearing chunky sweaters; and Melissa's small legs were encased in well-fitting jodhpurs. Her father was not wearing riding breeches, but his tight-fitting pants were thrust into knee-length black boots, and moulded the bulging muscles of his powerful thighs.

Alix didn't need to see the crop Melissa was carrying as she skipped lamely along beside her father to guess that they had been riding, and she wondered how many horses Oliver Morgan kept at the Hall. It was years since she had done any riding, but it was a tantalising prospect on a day that was doubtless as sharp and as clear as mountain air. Still, she thought half impatiently, she was not here to enjoy herself in any capacity, but she returned to the table with a certain amount of dissatisfaction.

She was still sitting there when the door swung open and her employer and his daughter entered the room. They brought with them the fresh tang of pine and larch, and even Melissa's naturally pale features were flushed with healthy colour.

'Good morning, Miss—I mean, Mrs Thornton,' she exclaimed excitedly. 'What are you doing?'

Oliver Morgan closed the door behind them. 'I believe your governess is preparing tomorrow's lessons, Melly,' he told her lightly before Alix could reply, his size successfully reducing the generous proportions of the room. In the revealing light of day the grey streaks in his hair were more pronounced, but for all that he was still the most disturbing man Alix had ever encountered.

'As a matter of fact, I've been reading, Melissa,' she said, deliberately addressing her remarks to the child. She lifted the book to show her. 'Do you know it?'

Melissa came to the table and studied the coloured jacket. Then she shook her head. 'No. The only books I've read are about Yoko.'

'Yoko?'

Alix frowned, and Oliver came to the table, hitching himself on to one corner and saying in mock-reproof: 'Yoko, the rabbit! Surely you've heard of him! He's quite a famous fellow, isn't he, Melly?'

Melissa giggled, and said: 'Oh, *Daddy*!' while Alix was amazed at his indulgence with the child. Whoever would have guessed that the unapproachable scourge of the Royal Academy could be so sensitive to a little girl's fantasies? He had been smiling teasingly at the child, but suddenly he turned and found her eyes upon him, and for a devastating minute he held her gaze. She was sure he did it deliberately, and only a determination not to give in to whatever egotistical urge he had to humiliate her forced her not to look away. Nevertheless, when Melissa did inevitably distract his attention, Alix felt exhausted by the effort.

Quickly tiring of the books, Melissa had more important things on her mind: 'We've been riding,' she told Alix eagerly. 'Can you ride, Mrs Thornton?'

Alix hesitated. 'Well, I used to ride years ago,' she conceded at last, and immediately Melissa looked up at her father and said:

'Perhaps Mrs Thornton could take me riding when you're working.'

'Oh, I don't know about that,' protested Alix doubtfully, aware of Oliver's eyes on her again. 'I mean—it's years since I was on a horse.'

'It's like swimming, Mrs Thornton. You don't forget,' remarked her employer dryly. 'However, if you would care to join us next time we go riding. . .'

Melissa looked less enthusiastic about this, and

Alix surmised that the little girl did not have so much of her father's attention that she was prepared to dilute it. 'Perhaps if you could direct me to the stables, I could try a mount some time,' she suggested casually, and Oliver slid abruptly off the desk to face them.

'We'll see,' he said curtly, his eyes dropping to his daughter's dark head. 'Well, poppet, this is where I leave you.' His eyes flicked coldly over Alix. 'I'm sure you'll be quite adequately cared for in Mrs Thornton's capable hands.'

'Oh, Daddy. . .' Melissa was dismayed. 'I thought we were going to have milk and biscuits together.'

'Mrs Thornton will share your milk and biscuits, Melly. Far more enthusiastically than me, I do assure you,' he responded dryly, and Alix could feel embarrassment sweeping over her.

'But, Daddy—'

Her father's features hardened, and Alix recognised the signs. 'I have work to do, Melly,' he said inflexibly. 'You know that. I warned you what it would be like before I brought you here. . .'

'I know you did.' Melissa hunched her thin shoulders. 'All right, all right. Go and do your work. I'll stay here with Mrs Thornton.'

'Good girl.' Briefly his hand descended on her head, the long brown fingers caressing. Then he inclined his head towards Alix, and strode swiftly out of the room.

There was a moment's silence after he had gone when Melissa looked as if she was going to cry, but then she bravely held up her head and said: 'I'm glad you've come here, Mrs Thornton. It will be nice having someone young to talk to.'

Alix felt more relaxed now that Oliver Morgan was no longer in the room. 'Well, I hope we can talk to each other, Melissa,' she said gently, and then felt a twinge of conscience for the innocence of the child.

Melissa came round the table and perched on the arm of Alix's chair. Considering her parentage, she was remarkably unselfconscious, and Alix could only guess that the elderly Miss Stanwick was responsible for her uncomplicated disposition.

'Tell me about London,' she said, carelessly flicking over the textbooks, and Alix's eyes widened.

'I thought you were going to help me with preparing tomorrow's lessons!' she protested good-humouredly, and the little girl pulled a face.

'Must I? Couldn't we just talk together?' she pleaded, and Alix discovered she was not immune to the appeal of ingenuously curving lips and eyes that danced with mischief.

'What do you want to know about London?' she yielded with wry humour, and Melissa clasped her hands.

'Everything,' she said dramatically. 'I want to go there soon, but Daddy says I have to go to school first. He used to live there, you know. He had a house, too, but I believe he liked living in London best. He's a sculptor, you know. He's very clever!'

'I know.' Alix's tone was dry, but Melissa didn't notice it.

'He can draw too,' the child went on. 'He's drawn me—lots of times. And he says he's going to make a—a—well, he's going to do my head. Just for himself.'

Alix bit her lip. 'You're a lucky girl,' she commented, and Melissa nodded, leaving the chair to cover the width of the room with her half-skipping step.

'I know,' she said, halting before the fireplace, then she sighed. 'What a pity Miss Stanwick had to die. She wanted to come back to England so badly.'

Alix stacked the textbooks together. 'You cared for Miss Stanwick, didn't you?' she observed quietly.

'Oh, yes,' Melissa nodded. 'She was very kind. She used to talk to me for hours and hours.'

Alix's tongue dampened her upper lip. 'Did—did Miss Stanwick know your mother, Melissa?' she asked, but the child wasn't listening to her.

'She used to tell me what England was like when she was a little girl,' she went on solemnly. 'She was very old.'

'Did she live in London too?' Alix queried, deciding there was no point in trying to rush things. Confidence had to be given, not asked for.

'I think so,' answered Melissa, frowning, 'some of the time anyway. Her daddy was a parson. They used to live in a big old house, not at all like this one. She said it was always cold, and she and her sisters used to snuggle together in bed to keep warm.' She paused. 'She had seven brothers and sisters! I wish I did.'

Alix had no answer to that, but fortunately Melissa didn't appear to expect one. 'Miss Stanwick said that when they used to go shopping, they had to go in a horse and cart. There were no motor cars in those days, you know, and all the ladies wore long dresses.' She hesitated a moment before adding: 'Do you wish you wore long dresses, Mrs Thornton?'

'I do sometimes,' answered Alix easily. 'Nowadays, girls often wear long dresses.'

'In the evenings?'

'And during the day as well,' Alix insisted, guessing where this conversation was leading. 'Anything is acceptable these days.'

'In London?'

'Everywhere.'

Melissa looked doubtful. 'I'd like to wear long dresses all the time,' she said, 'then people wouldn't be able to see my legs.'

Alix got to her feet. 'What's wrong with your legs? They look very pretty legs to me.'

Melissa wrinkled her nose. 'Oh—you *know*! One of them is shorter than the other.'

Alix shook her head. 'That's not such an insurmountable problem. Particularly not these days.'

'What do you mean?' Melissa's brow was furrowed.

'Well, take a look at my shoes,' said Alix, lifting her trouser leg to display the wedged sole. 'I'm sure you could get some shoes that wouldn't look so different from these. Then you'd be fashionable, as well.'

Melissa's eyes widened. 'Daddy said that, but I thought he was just teasing.'

'Oh, no,' Alix shook her head, 'I'm sure he meant it. Perhaps when you go to London. . .'

'Mmm.' Melissa nodded eagerly, her eyes brightening again.

Alix straightened her trousers, and asked casually: 'Is this your first visit to England, Melissa?' and the little girl nodded once more.

'Yes. I—I couldn't come before.'

'Why not?'

The question was out before Alix could prevent it, but the answer was lost when Mrs Brandon came into the library, carrying a tray containing a jug of milk and biscuits, and two glasses. She looked taken aback to find Alix with the child, and looked round questioningly for Oliver Morgan.

'Mr Morgan had some work to do, Mrs Brandon.' Alix had to say something. 'Melissa and I will share the milk, thank you.'

Mrs Brandon set the tray down on the table with obvious ill-grace. 'Mr Morgan asked for that specially, he did,' she said accusingly, almost as if Alix had denied him of it. 'What's he doing about lunch?'

Alix looked at Melissa, but the little girl merely shrugged, and it was left to her to disclaim all knowledge of Mr Morgan's plans.

'I expect he's gone and shut himself away in that hut again,' muttered the housekeeper irritably, 'not eating for days on end. It isn't good for him.'

'A hut!' Alix was bewildered now. 'I don't think—'

'Mrs Brandon means the north tower,' interposed Melissa suddenly. 'That's where Daddy works. He likes to be alone.'

'The north tower?' Alix shook her head. 'You mean the lodge?'

'No!' Mrs Brandon was scornful. 'That's Giles's cottage, that is. She means the old peel tower. It hasn't been used for years, leastways, not until Mr Morgan started using it. Falling to bits about his ears, it is.'

'Daddy likes it,' asserted Melissa, but her voice lacked conviction, and its tremor made Alix impatient with Mrs Brandon's lack of tact.

'I'm sure he does, Melissa,' she reassured her, and then looked again at the housekeeper. 'Does Mr Morgan usually return for lunch?'

'Sometimes—sometimes not.'

'Then I suggest you prepare something just in case,' said Alix firmly, and knew she had offended the woman again when she left the room without another word.

Melissa helped herself to a biscuit from the tray, but she still looked anxious. 'Old buildings can be dangerous, can't they?' she murmured doubtfully.

'Yes.' Alix saw no point in lying to her. 'But you don't imagine your father would take the trouble to bring you to England and then risk killing himself, do you?'

Melissa wanted to believe her. 'Don't you think so?'

'Well! Does it make sense to you?' demanded Alix, unwilling to admit the thought that not everything Oliver Morgan did was sensible. But at least, judging from his daughter's expression, her optimism had been justified.

'No,' Melissa agreed, biting into her biscuit. 'No, you're right, Mrs Thornton. Daddy wouldn't do anything so silly.' And then, more reflectively: 'Why doesn't Mrs Brandon like you?'

Alix poured the milk from the jug into the two glasses. 'She doesn't know me,' she countered evasively. 'Now drink this. Then you can tell me what Miss Stanwick used to teach you.'

Makoto appeared soon after twelve, to take Melissa to wash her hands before lunch. The little girl went with her with evident relief, and Alix knew that the concentration of the last hour had been a not altogether enjoyable experience for her. She was inclined to be lazy, and although she could read the exercises Alix set out for her, she preferred to doodle on a piece of paper with a pencil, or gaze dreamily out of the window. When she was forced to take an interest in what Alix was saying, she assumed a sulky expression, and it had taken all Alix's patience not to get annoyed with her. It was obvious that the elderly Miss Stanwick had preferred to take the easy way out with her, and Alix was amazed that she could read at all. But Melissa was an intelligent child, and no doubt that was how she could spell out words after the minimum amount of tuition.

They had the lunch table to themselves, as Alix and Oliver Morgan had had the evening before. Alix had expected Makoto to join them for the meal, but when she mentioned this to Melissa, she looked surprised.

'Oh, no,' she exclaimed, with unconscious hauteur. 'Makoto is only a servant.'

'I suppose you could say the same of me,' remarked Alix dryly, not particularly caring for the distinction, and Melissa had the grace to look shamefaced.

'Makoto wouldn't want to eat at the table,' she protested, waving her knife in the air to impress the point. 'In Japan you sit on the floor, on cushions, and Makoto would feel out of place at a table like this.'

'But you don't,' remarked Alix, forking smoked salmon into her mouth, and Melissa shook her head.

'Miss Stanwick—'

'I know,' Alix interrupted her. 'Miss Stanwick insisted on sitting at an ordinary table.'

Melissa's eyes danced. 'Yes. How did you know?'

Alix shook her head, her lips curving wryly. 'I really have no idea,' she answered teasingly, and Melissa giggled.

It was a pleasant meal, although Alix was conscious that her employer could appear at any time. However, he did not return, but when the meal was over she was surprised when Makoto arrived and shepherded Melissa out of the room. Leaving her coffee, Alix went after them to ask what was going on.

'Missy must rest, Thornton *san*,' the tiny Japanese woman explained politely. 'Tea is served at four o'clock.'

'Four o'clock!' Alix was exasperated. She looked at Melissa. 'You don't mean to tell me you rest until four o'clock!'

'It's only two hours, Mrs Thornton,' the little girl answered in surprise. 'I always rest in the afternoons.'

'In Japan perhaps,' protested Alix impatiently, 'but not here, in England! You're not an invalid, Melissa. You don't need that much rest!'

Makoto began to urge the child upstairs, and short of dragging her back again there was nothing Alix could do. Melissa cast a half-apologetic look over her shoulder, but she obviously wasn't opposed to her normal practice, and Alix guessed that the prospect of more lessons would not be a persuasion.

The two small figures disappeared along the corridor leading to the east wing, and Alix pushed her hands into the waistline pockets of her pants. What now? The whole afternoon stretched ahead of her. One thing was certain—she was not going to be overworked here.

She wandered into the library again, but she had examined all the textbooks, and she had a fair idea of the kind of approach she would have to make to gain Melissa's interest. A pale sun filtered its rays across the russet-coloured carpet, and on impulse she turned out of the room again and ran upstairs to collect her coat. No one had said she should not explore, and the idea of getting out into the fresh air was appealing.

Seth appeared as she was opening the heavy front door, and he hurried to help her with it. She hadn't seen him since the previous evening, and she decided that none of the staff at Darkwater Hall could complain of arduous working conditions.

'Are you going out, Mrs Thornton?' he asked, rather unnecessarily, she felt, and when she explained that she was going for a walk, he said: 'I'll telephone

Giles and let him know you're in the grounds.'

Alix was standing at the top of the steps, putting up the collar of her sheepskin coat against an unexpected chill in the air, and she turned to look at him disbelievingly: 'You'll *what*?'

'The dogs, Mrs Thornton,' explained the old man patiently. 'You'd not want to be meeting them on your walk, now would you?'

Alix licked her lips. 'They're not dangerous. Giles said. . .'

'They're watchdogs, Mrs Thornton.'

'But Mr Morgan—'

'—knows them, Mrs Thornton. Have a pleasant walk.'

The door was closed behind her and Alix went half reluctantly down the steps. It was disconcerting to realise that there was no way she could leave Darkwater Hall without alerting someone to her intentions. As if the length of the drive wasn't deterrent enough!

Shrugging these thoughts aside, she pushed her hands into the pockets of her coat and began to walk across the gravelled forecourt. Now that she could see the whole of the Hall, it was possible to distinguish between the central portion and the two wings, which had probably been added some years after the main building had been erected. The stark grey walls had been overlaid with creeper, its rusty autumn colouring giving warmth to the stone, and in spite of its size it had lost much of that brooding air of mystery it had possessed in the fog. It was simply a rather charming country house, with all the grace of line and structure of a bygone age.

A path between dripping rhododendron bushes, brought her round to the back of the house. She could see the tall windows of the library, and the terrace she had glimpsed from them earlier. As she progressed along the path beside the rose garden she began to realise that beyond the narrow barrier of trees there were more buildings and outhouses, and she guessed that this was where the horses were stabled. She was tempted to go and introduce herself to whoever cared for the horses, but she wasn't dressed for riding, and besides, Oliver Morgan might not like her intruding without invitation.

Skirting the stables, she emerged from the trees upon rolling parkland, deserted save for a few sheep cropping the stubby turf. Here and there, wooded copses broke up the open landscape, but Alix's chief impression was one of splendid isolation.

Some yards further on tyre tracks scarred the sweep of green, muddy trenches worn deep into the earth. They seemed to come from the direction of the stables, and continued on down a slope and up the other side, disappearing into another small wood. On impulse Alix decided to follow them, but she was breathless by the time she had climbed the knoll, which was steeper than she had thought. She leant against the bole of a tree to recover, and started violently when something leapt away from her and went bounding into the shadows. The realisation that it had been a wild deer brought a warm feeling of incredulity, and she straightened to stare regretfully after the timid creature.

The wood was thick with fallen leaves, and she realised it would be impossible to distinguish any more tyre tracks with the sun rapidly fading and darkness creeping inexorably nearer. Breathing an impatient sigh, she turned back, wishing it was spring, not autumn. But at least her afternoon had passed quite pleasantly, and this evening she would tackle Oliver Morgan about some changes in Melissa's timetable now that she had a governess.

CHAPTER FOUR

BUT Alix's plans of talking to Oliver Morgan were doomed to frustration. When she came down for dinner it was to find that the dining table was set for only one, and Mrs Brandon was quick to explain that Mr Morgan had returned earlier on in the afternoon, while Alix was out walking, and had informed her that he would not be in to dinner.

'Took some food back with him, he did,' she continued, supplying Alix with pâté to spread on wafer-thin slices of toast. 'I think he'd expected to speak to you, but as you weren't here. . .'

Alix pressed her lips tightly together. 'Thank you, Mrs Brandon.'

The housekeeper looked maliciously amused. 'Not much fun for you, is it?' she jeered. 'I bet this wasn't what you expected when you offered to come up here.'

Alix put down her knife. She had had just about enough of Mrs Brandon's insinuations. 'I came here to do a job of work, Mrs Brandon,' she stated coldly, controlling the almost irresistible urge to slap the older woman's sneering face. 'Mr Morgan's activities do not interest me, except insofar as they affect my relationship with his daughter. I suggest you keep your unsubtle innuendoes for people like yourself who appreciate them!'

'Now, you look here—'

'No, you look here,' Alix warmed to her task. 'If as you say, my association with your employer does go beyond those bounds, what's stopping me from going straight to him with your accusations? Surely he couldn't approve of you baiting his girl-friends!'

Mrs Brandon's mouth worked silently for a few moments. 'Mr Morgan's not been in the habit of bringing his girl-friends here!' she muttered.

'In the habit?' Alix frowned. Then, realising she was not supposed to know anything of her employer's history, she added: 'I mean—does he spend a lot of time here?'

Mrs Brandon shrugged. 'Three or four months every year,' she conceded unthinkingly. And then with a return of hostility: 'What's it to you?'

'Oh, nothing.' Alix shook her head, realising that the purchase of Darkwater Hall had not been the recent innovation she had thought. 'It—well, it just seems so far from London.'

'That's why he likes it,' asserted the housekeeper. 'Keeps them reporters at bay. Always poking around, they are, trying to dig up gossip about him. Fair makes you sick the way they hounded him after his wife's death!'

Alix endeavoured to appear unmoved by what Mrs Brandon was saying. This was one source of information she had never expected to tap, and if the housekeeper so much as suspected that Alix was interested in what she was saying, she would never utter another word.

'I—I suppose they have a job to do,' she ventured

at last, and Mrs Brandon gave an angry snort.

'What kind of a job is that!'

Alix spread pâté with slightly unsteady fingers. 'Don't you approve of freedom of the press, Mrs Brandon?'

'No, I don't. Not when it means people can't live their lives in peace and privacy.'

Alix chose her words carefully. 'But surely you have to admit that some things deserve publicity. I mean—well, just think of all the corruption that's been exposed—'

'Who decides what's corruption and what's not?' demanded the housekeeper, folding her arms. 'It seems to me there's something corrupt about them people who work for the newspapers, pushing their noses into other people's affairs, making their lives a misery!'

Alix hesitated. 'I suppose the answer to that is that if you have nothing to hide, you have nothing to fear,' she said.

Mrs Brandon looked suspicious. 'And you think Mr Morgan has something to hide, is that it?'

'*No!*' Alix was horrified. 'I didn't say that. We were talking in purely general terms.'

'Huh!' The housekeeper was still sceptical. 'Well, don't you go thinking you'll be able to boast about living here when you get back to London. Mr Morgan won't have that.'

Alix was tempted to ask how he could stop it, but that would have been foolish; so instead she concentrated on the painting over the sideboard, deciding that Mrs Brandon was not about to make any more revelations this evening.

The meal progressed through roast beef and Yorkshire pudding, followed by a fruit salad, to the coffee stage, and refusing cheese and crackers, as she had done the night before, Alix carried her coffee into the library. She was less conscious of her solitary confinement in here, and she curled up on the couch and gazed into the fire.

It had been a curiously unsatisfying day, although she couldn't altogether blame Melissa for that. Nevertheless, when she returned from her walk, it had been rather galling to find the child upstairs in her sitting room, taking tea with Makoto, with obviously no intention of attending any more lessons that day. That had been another of the reasons she had wanted to speak to Oliver Morgan, and she wondered whether the following day would follow the same pattern. Without his intervention, she didn't see how she could alter it.

But it wasn't just that which was making her restless. Her walk this afternoon had demonstrated to her how cut off from the outside world she was, and she still had no idea how she was going to make contact with Willie. What could she do? The only telephone she had seen was in the hall, with audible access to anyone passing through, and she wouldn't trust either Mrs Brandon or her daughter not to listen in to any call she might make. She had no car, no transport of any kind; and she couldn't even walk to the gates without first having Giles call off the dogs. Besides, the nearest village was almost three miles away, and her footwear had not been bought for hiking. She wondered if Oliver Morgan ever left the premises when he was in residence, or would that constitute a betrayal of his anonymity? If he had wanted to create a fortress here, he could not have done so with more success.

Surprisingly, Alix slept well that night. Her walk in the grounds must have been more tiring than she had thought, and not even the wind, which stirred in the early morning hours and tossed the shadows of skeletal branches across her windows, disturbed her.

She awakened soon after seven, and not willing to relax again and possibly oversleep, she got up and took a long, leisurely bath. Deciding her style of apparel was not important, she wore her favourite denim jeans and a red and white striped sweater, hesitating briefly over whether or not she ought to wear a bra. The ribbed lines of the sweater were very revealing, but as only Melissa was likely to see her, she gave in to her preference not to do so.

It was a little after eight when she went downstairs, and when she went into the dining room, she found the table had not yet been laid. Obviously Mrs Brandon had had no faith in her determination not to oversleep, and wanting to show that she was indeed up and waiting for her breakfast, Alix crossed to the door which led to the kitchens at the back of the house. A short passage ended in a baize-covered swing door, which gave with the lightest pressure of her fingers into the stone-flagged kitchen. It might have been a cold room had it not been for the enormous Aga stove pulsing out heat in the corner, but

Alix was less concerned with her surroundings than with the man seated carelessly at the scrubbed wooden table, eating a plate of ham and eggs. She had not expected to find Oliver Morgan here, of all places, and she was immediately conscious of her intrusion, and the casualness of her attire.

He looked up at her entrance, and his eyes registered his surprise at her appearance. Perhaps he had expected Myra, as neither she nor her mother was in the room, or perhaps it was simply irritation that caused the sudden flare of anger that tightened his lips.

'I'm sorry,' she said when he made no move to get up and greet her, 'I was looking for Mrs Brandon.'

'She's putting some laundry in the machine,' Oliver Morgan told her shortly, taking a gulp of tea from the mug beside him. 'She won't be long. Do you want breakfast?'

'I—' Alix hovered by the half-open door. 'Not what you're having.'

'No?' His eyes were coldly mocking. 'I thought you enjoyed your food.'

Alix stiffened. 'Aren't you being rather personal, Mr Morgan?'

'I don't see how I can be anything else, in the circumstances,' he retorted dryly, his eyes frankly assessing. 'You're a big girl, Mrs Thornton. You can take it, I'm sure.'

Alix's fists clenched. 'Will you tell Mrs Brandon I'll have some toast and coffee when she's ready—'

'Just a minute.' Oliver Morgan pushed his plate aside and rose to his feet, tall and powerful in hip-hugging cream cords, stained with paint and what might be plaster, and a denim shirt that gaped across his chest. 'There's plenty of toast here, if you want it, and the percolator's bubbling on the stove. That is unless the kitchen's not good enough for you.'

'The kitchen has nothing to do with it,' retorted Alix coldly. 'But I prefer not to indulge your sarcastic sense of humour any longer!'

He eyed her narrowly, moving his head in a gesture of indifference. 'As you will.'

Alix sighed, and half turned away, but as he was subsiding into his seat again, she asked tentatively: 'Will you be in to lunch or dinner today?'

He stretched his long legs beneath the table. 'Is it essential that I should be?'

Alix wished she could tell him no. But she had to make the effort to speak to him.

'I—er—I'd like to discuss Melissa's timetable with you.' she replied stiffly. 'And—and what hours off I'm to be given.'

He rested his elbows on the table, and ran his hands round the back of his neck, under the untidy length of his hair. 'I see.' He looked her way. 'I thought we dealt with all that.'

'I don't think so.'

'Your time's your own after four o'clock, Mrs Thornton. And naturally you won't work weekends, I appreciate that. What more do you want?'

Alix sighed. 'It's not just that, Mr Morgan.'

'Then goddammit, what is it?' He got up from the table again, and for an awful moment she thought he was going to strike her. 'Look, Mrs Thornton, I meant it yesterday when I said I had work to do. I have a piece I have to get finished before Christmas, and I thought that by bringing you here I was getting some-one who could cope!'

'I can cope,' she exclaimed indignantly, stung by his tone. 'At least, when I know what it is I have to cope with!'

He glared at her. 'What's that supposed to mean?'

Alix unconsciously squared her shoulders. 'There are—complications I have to discuss with you, Mr Morgan. If we could arrange an appointment—'

'To hell with appointments! I don't make appoint-ments, Mrs Thornton. If you have something to say come right out and say it, for God's sake!'

Alix hesitated. 'I—I'd prefer to speak to you pri-vately,' she insisted.

He shook his head irritably, flinging out a hand to indicate the chair across the table from his. 'Why can't you come and sit down and have some breakfast and talk to me now? I promise I won't indulge my sarcastic sense of humour!'

'Mrs Brandon will be back at any minute. You said so.'

His eyes narrowed. 'It's that private, eh?'

Alix wished he hadn't the power to embarrass her so easily. With a little shrug she turned away, saying tautly: 'I'll speak to you when you have more time, Mr Morgan,' and the door swung to behind her.

He came after her as she had half expected he would. But she refused to stay in the room and listen to more of his scarcely-veiled insults, and she was crossing the hall to the stairs when his voice halted her.

'You'd better come into my study, Mrs Thornton,' he commanded harshly, and she looked round to find him opening a door to the right of the stairs. It was a room which hitherto Alix had not entered, but like the library opposite, it possessed a similar intimacy, enhanced by mellow panelled walls and the smell of leather. It was obvious that fires were burned here, too, although at present the grate was screened, and only the adequate heating system took away the chill. A leather-topped desk stood by the windows which overlooked the drive, faced on either side by soft, hide-covered chairs, but Oliver Morgan ignored these and merely draped his leg over a corner of the desk. Folding his arms, he waited for her to close the door, and then said grimly: 'Well?'

Alix faced him reluctantly. 'You're making this very difficult for me,' she said.

'Why?' He was unmoved by her diffidence. 'This is what you wanted, isn't it?'

Alix sighed. 'Hardly.'

'What do you mean?'

'I haven't even had a cup of coffee yet,' she protested.

'You were offered one.'

Alix's temper came to her rescue. 'Does it give you some kind of sadistic pleasure to bait people?' she asked, and his lips thinned.

'Is that what you wanted to ask me?'

'No. No, of course not.'

'Then I suggest you get to the point.'

'You have a strange way of inspiring confidence in your employees, don't you, Mr Morgan?' she demanded.

His legs came down off the desk with a thud, and he straightened. 'What is your problem, Mrs Thornton? I do not have the time or the inclination to stand here arguing my hang-ups. Do you or do you not have something you wish to say to me?'

Alix shifted her weight from one foot to the other: 'Yes.'

'Go on.'

She waited a moment, and then she said: 'What can I do when Makoto insists that Melissa rests every afternoon?'

He was silent for several seconds, and then he nodded his head slowly. 'It's true, Melissa always has rested in the afternoon.'

'And is she to go on doing so?'

He shook his head impatiently. 'I haven't thought about it.'

'Then perhaps you should. She's not a baby, Mr Morgan, and England is not Japan.'

'I know that.' He looked frustrated, and he paced restlessly across to the hearth and back before speaking again. 'Of course, this interferes with your time for lessons.'

'Yes.'

He paused. 'How did Melissa react to you after I'd left yesterday?'

Alix shrugged. 'Socially, very well. Academically, not so enthusiastically. I don't think she's used to—to—'

'Discipline?' Alix agreed, and he nodded his head. 'She's not. Much as I liked Miss Stanwick, I was always aware of her limitations: that was one of the reasons why I wanted to bring Melissa back to England.' He halted then as though regretting he had said so much, and when he spoke again, it was much less openly. 'I will speak to Makoto—and Melissa.'

'If you explain that when she goes to school she won't be able to rest in the afternoons—' began Alix, only to be silenced again by his sardonic stare.

'I know how to phrase the matter,' he retorted shortly. 'I am not without tact where my daughter is concerned.'

Alix flushed. 'I never said you were.'

'The implication was there.' He hesitated. 'Was there something else?'

'Yes.' Alix hated having to bring anything else up with him in this mood. 'The problem of my free time.'

'That's a problem?'

She sighed. 'Leaving the Hall is.'

'The grounds, you mean?' His eyes narrowed speculatively. 'You want to leave the grounds?'

'Is that so unreasonable?'

He shrugged. 'Where would you go? The village—Bridleburn—is a quiet community. There's only one store, and even the children are taken some distance to school. Newcastle, as you know, is more than thirty miles away.'

'There are buses,' she told him quickly, and he inclined his head.

'Yes, there are. But I shouldn't rely on them when the weather gets bad.'

'Are you suggesting that I don't leave the Hall?' she demanded, aware of an increasing feeling of chill.

'I'm suggesting that you make use of the facilities we have here in your spare time,' he told her evenly. 'The grounds are extensive. You can go for walks, you can ride; there are books and television—'

'It sounds suspiciously like a prison to me!' she retorted, hiding her unease.

He frowned. 'I am sure the conditions here were explained to you before you left London. Grizelda—Lady Morgan—had strict orders that she must stress the point of the isolation.'

'She did. But—'

He made an irritated gesture. 'I go into Newcastle myself approximately once a month. If you're so desperate for activity, you may accompany me.'

Alix trembled. A concession, at last. The prisoner was accompanied by an escort! 'I—is there some reason why I shouldn't make my own way there?' she queried carefully. 'Providing I'm prepared to risk the uncertainty of the buses?'

Oliver's frown deepened. 'You seem uncommonly eager to show your independence, Mrs Thornton. I'm beginning to suspect your relationship with your husband may not be as distant as you would have me believe.'

'That has nothing to do with it,' she said sharply.

'Then what has?'

'I—I just think I ought to be able to come and go as I please.'

'I see.' His grey eyes narrowed between thick lashes, 'And what guarantee would I have that you might not go rushing to the nearest telephone to contact some newspaper in London?'

Alix swallowed the gasp that almost escaped her. 'I—contact some newspaper in London!' she echoed faintly. 'Wh—why would I do that?'

His sigh was an angry expellation of his breath. 'I do not believe you're that naïve, Mrs Thornton,' he snapped. 'You know damn well why it could be in your interests to do so. I explained the situation when you came here, and you must know what the gutter press would pay to learn of Melissa's existence!'

It was worse than she had imagined, and she had to thrust her hands into the pockets of her jeans to prevent him from seeing how they were trembling. 'And—and you think I would do that?' she stammered.

'I don't know, Mrs Thornton. I'll give you the benefit of the doubt and say that I don't know you well enough yet to gauge what you might do. But since I married Joanne—and God knows what a disaster that turned out to be—I have become somewhat of a pariah in press circles. I admit, I don't suffer fools gladly, and in spite of the fact that I put up with a good deal of inconvenience, I don't honestly see why being a sculptor pre-empts my right to live my life as I want it. But I accept. . .and you may even have noticed. . .' his lips twisted wryly, '. . .that I am not the most patient of men, and in consequence I have made enemies. Some of them in Fleet Street. That's why I have to make these conditions.

Melissa's happiness must always come first.'

Alix digested this with difficulty. 'But—I have to write to—to my family. . .'

He inclined his head sardonically. 'Naturally, you'll tell them that you're getting on well with the cataloguing of the library.'

'And if I refuse to lie about it?'

'I hope you won't.'

'Oh, but this is archaic!' she exclaimed.

'On the contrary, this situation would not have existed even a hundred years ago.'

Alix clenched her fists. 'And—and what if I choose to leave? What if I resign?'

He turned to look out of the windows. 'Why would you want to do that, Mrs Thornton? The salary is more than generous, I do know that, and your working conditions are hardly arduous. What possible reason could you have for wanting to leave?'

Alix shook her head helplessly. 'It—it's just the—the feeling of being cut off.'

'Hardly that. There's a telephone.' His eyes grew lazily mocking. 'You miss the company of—men, perhaps?'

'I didn't say that!'

'No,' he agreed, 'but all this indignation—there has to be a reason.'

'My reasons are as I've stated. I—if that's all, Mr Morgan, I'd like some breakfast.'

He left the windows to come and stand in front of her, and it took all her determination not to flee before the penetration of that speculative stare.

'I wonder why Grizelda sent *you* here,' he murmured, half to himself, and she didn't need the quickening of her own breathing to know that his earlier irritation had given way to an equally disturbing curiosity.

'Not—not everyone wanted to come and live so far away from London,' she stammered in reply, and his eyes darkened to the colour of wet slate.

'But you did!' he observed softly. 'Why? Have I got it all wrong? Are you running away from that husband of yours?'

'*No!*' Alix didn't know how long she could sustain this conversation. 'Well, thank you for giving me—'

'Seth tells me you went walking yesterday,' he continued as if she hadn't spoken, and she wondered if anything happened here without his being aware of it. But she nodded her head, and he looked thoughtful. 'You won't get lost, will you?' he probed. 'Darkwater covers a deal of ground, and I should hate you to fall into the pool.'

'The pool?' Alix frowned, curious in spite of herself. . .

'Darkwater Pool, from which the Hall derives its name. It's been here for a great number of years, and nobody seems to know how deep it is. I should imagine it's known its share of secrets in its time.'

Alix had been listening intently, but when she looked up and encountered his mocking gaze, resentment stirred inside her. 'What you're really saying is—don't stray off the reservation, aren't you, Mr Morgan?' she exclaimed bitterly.

'No. You couldn't do that, Mrs Thornton,' he retorted pleasantly. 'And my concern was genuine.

The pool used to have quite a notorious reputation before the land was fenced off, and I should hate to think of you struggling out of your depth with no one there to save you.'

'Where is the pool?' she asked reluctantly.

'I'll show you some time. When you've learned not to mistrust everything I say.'

Alix took a step backward. 'I don't mistrust everything you say,' she protested. 'Just because I was curious about my confinement here. . .'

'You're a contradiction, Mrs Thornton!' he told her wryly. 'You're not like any married woman I've ever known. What went wrong between you two? Was he impotent?'

Alix's face burned. 'How—how dare you suggest—'

He shrugged. 'I apologise,' he said flatly. 'I shouldn't have said that. And now as you seem determined to impugn my best motives, I suggest you run along and have your breakfast like the immaculate young woman you are!'

Contrarily, she felt let down when he turned away, his lean, hawklike features already registering other emotions than the momentary interest he had shown in her. But what did she expect, after all? she asked herself impatiently, as she walked into the dining room. A man of Oliver Morgan's age and experience did not play around with immature young women like herself, and she had momentarily amused him, nothing more.

But as she sipped her orange juice, Alix couldn't help wondering what he must have been like when he was younger, perhaps even twenty years younger. If he was attractive now, what must he have been like then? But the answer, extraordinary though it might be, was simply that then he had been a boy. Now he was a man. . .

CHAPTER FIVE

MELISSA appeared for lessons soon after nine. She was alone, which was unusual, and when she came into the library where Alix was waiting for her, her eyes looked puffed and swollen, as if she had been weeping. But her hair was stiffly braided, and her skirt and sweater were neatly pressed, and she slid into her seat beside Alix without a word.

Alix glanced at the child uncertainly, and noting the tightly clenched lips, decided not to make any personal comment. Instead she produced an exercise book, and passing it across to Melissa, said: 'We'll start with some spellings. Just easy words at first, until we see how clever you really are.'

Melissa took the book and pencil, and opened it obediently. Alix got to her feet, and moved across the room. 'Ready?' she asked, and when the child nodded, she began.

Ten minutes later Melissa handed her book over for marking. It was a mess of smudges and crossings out, but more importantly, not one of the simple words Alix had given her was spelt correctly. Alix's lips tightened when she realised that some words which had originally been set out correctly had been altered with wrong letters, so that it was obvious that Melissa knew exactly what she was doing.

Realising that psychology was needed here, Alix

laid the exercise book down on the table. 'Yes,' she said, nodding, 'very good.' She paused, allowing her words to sink in. 'Now we'll go on to arithmetic, shall we?'

Melissa looked as though she was going to protest, but then she shrugged her slim shoulders and accepted a second exercise book. Alix opened the textbook and indicated the first simple test. 'I'll give you ten minutes for those,' she said, and without much confidence moved away.

Melissa laid down her pencil at the end of five minutes, and Alix came back to the table. The ten questions had been answered, but as before, with the wrong figure.

Alix studied the book silently for a few minutes, feeling a rising sense of irritation. After all, she had not wanted to teach the child; that had not been her condition of employment. Indeed, she wondered again whether anyone faced with a similar situation might not have backed out at the last moment. Librarians were not teachers; they had had no experience in dealing with children, problem or otherwise, and she wasn't even a librarian!

But when she looked up into Melissa's grave little face, another idea struck her. Of course, why hadn't she thought of it before? If the child knew how to answer her questions wrongly, it followed that she must know the right answers, too.

She frowned. But how far could anyone go on that premise? When would she know whether Melissa knew the right answers or not? She tapped a nail against her teeth. When she started getting them right, she supposed. In any case, with luck it might not get that far. Surely there would come a time when Melissa would want to show what she could do!

Now, as before, she nodded and complimented the little girl on the speed with which she had accomplished the test. She deliberately kept her tone light, and ignored the way Melissa's mouth drooped when it became apparent that Alix was not going to get angry with her. It was as if she wanted to be scolded: but why? So that she could go rushing to her father with stories of Alix's cruelty? Obviously he had spoken to his daughter as he said he would, but what had he said to make her behave in this way? She was a different child from the smiling little girl Alix had encountered on her first evening at the Hall, and she didn't understand why.

The rest of the morning Alix spent in sketching a map of England and showing Melissa exactly where they were on it. She hoped she might gain the child's interest, that she might begin to make progress, but Melissa viewed all her efforts with the same indifference. Only when she read to her did the little girl's eyes light up, and she listened eagerly to the first of Roald Dahl's stories about Charlie Bucket, and almost looked disappointed when Mrs Brandon came to tell them that lunch was ready.

As on the previous day, there were only the two of them at the table. Myra served them, but she only spoke to Melissa, and so it was left to Alix to introduce topics of conversation.

'Have you seen your father this morning, Melissa?' she asked, offering her the plate of chicken broth which she had just served from the tureen.

'I don't want any soup, thank you,' asserted Melissa, folding her hands in her lap, and Alix bit her tongue as she lowered the soup dish in front of herself.

While she drank the soup, Alix was conscious of Melissa's eyes upon her, but she refused to let a child see that she had the power to disturb her, and she deliberately took a second helping to show her that she was not hurting anyone but herself by her awkwardness.

There was fish to follow, and Alix had to admit it looked delicious surrounded by curls of creamed potato, covered by a savoury sauce flavoured with parsley. She offered the dish to Melissa first, deciding to let her help herself this time, but again the little girl refused to take any food and Alix began to feel tension causing a tender ache in the region of her temples.

Trying not to get upset, she helped herself from the silver dish, but her taste for the food was waning as her headache increased. After all, she thought resentfully, she was not used to this kind of blackmail—or any kind of blackmail, for that matter. Melissa was just seeing how far she could go, and if she showed that the child was getting through to her, she might as well give up here and now. She had to remember that Melissa was her father's child, even though dumb insolence had never been his trademark.

Alix refused dessert, and was not entirely surprised when Melissa decided to have some of the lemon meringue pie Myra set on the table. In fact she had three helpings, but when Mrs Brandon brought in the coffee she slipped lightly off her chair.

Immediately Alix was on her feet, uncaring that the housekeeper was watching them. 'Where do you think you're going?'

Melissa's lips pursed for a moment, and then she said steadily: 'I want to use the lavatory.'

Alix's fingers tightened on the back of her chair. 'Oh! Well, couldn't you at least say "Excuse me", Melissa?'

'All right.' The child shrugged. 'Excuse me.'

Alix had to let her go. Short of accompanying her to the bathroom, there was nothing else she could do, and she subsided into her seat again, not unaware of Mrs Brandon's malicious satisfaction at her defeat.

She had drunk three cups of coffee before she realised that it was over half an hour since Melissa had disappeared. Pushing back her chair, she left the table and walked into the library. She had not really expected to find the child there, and she was not disappointed. But the fact remained that Melissa had to be somewhere.

The obvious places to look, of course, were her rooms in the east wing, and Alix ran quickly up the stairs, not halting until she came to the door at the end of the corridor. Makoto answered her knock, as she had expected she would, but when she asked for Melissa the Japanese woman shook her head.

'Missy taking lessons all afternoon,' she told Alix, with a stiff bow. 'Morgan *san* say Missy does not need to rest every day.'

Alix took a deep breath. 'I know that, but she's disappeared.' She sighed. 'She left me to go to the bathroom.'

Makoto shook her head, her hands folded into the sleeves of the inevitable kimono. There was that inscrutable eastern look about her which hitherto Alix had never actually believed in, but Makoto was a fine example of implacability.

'So she's not here?' she persisted, and Makoto shook her head. 'Do you know where she is?'

Again the tiny Japanese woman shook her head, and Alix turned resignedly away. She couldn't altogether be sure that Melissa wasn't hiding in her rooms somewhere, that she might not have put Makoto up to lying to her. But would the old servant disobey Morgan *san*'s instructions? With a sigh she conceded that she had no real way of knowing.

There were dozens of rooms where Melissa could be hiding, of course, but Alix had no intention of spending the whole afternoon searching for her. If Melissa wanted to play games, she could play them alone. She was going back to the library, and if the child wasn't there, she would find something to read, and relax.

But Melissa *was* there, sitting curled up on the couch, reading the book Alix had been reading to her earlier. Alix could feel her nails digging into her palms, but Melissa's disappointment when she appeared made up a little for her wasted efforts. Obviously the child had expected her to look everywhere for her before coming back to the library, and she scrambled to her feet sulkily, limping to her chair at the table.

Alix forced a smile, realising that she had won this particular skirmish, and then, glancing towards the brisk autumn day outside, she said: 'We're going for a nature ramble this afternoon. Go and get your coat while I speak to Seth.'

For once Melissa looked taken aback. 'Do you mean—we're going for a walk?' she asked in astonishment.

'That's right.'

'But I don't—that is—' Melissa looked down at her lame leg. 'I mean—I never walk anywhere.'

'Then perhaps it's time you did,' asserted Alix cheerfully, her tension rapidly dispersing. 'Go along, get your coat. I'll meet you in the hall in five minutes.'

Melissa went, surprisingly enough, and she was waiting in the hall, small and attractive in a fur-lined red cape, when Alix came down the stairs buttoning her sheepskin jacket. 'Red Riding Hood,' she commented, and Melissa looked pleased.

Outside, the air was crisp with just a trace of frost, and Seth, who had agreed to warn Giles of their outing, expressed the view that they would have snow before too long.

'Snow!' exclaimed Alix in amazement. 'In November?'

'We've had it in October before now,' the old man assured her severely. 'You're not in the south of England now, you know. This is border country.'

'I know.' She was able to smile without effort.

Adjusting her pace to Melissa's, Alix directed their steps in the opposite direction from that which she had taken the day before. The idea of a country walk had been an inspiration, and judging from the little girl's expression, she had almost forgotten her earlier obstructiveness. They crossed a field, and a small wood, and when they found a rabbit hole, Melissa insisted she had seen a tawny shadow slipping away into the undergrowth. Whether or not it had been a fox was debatable, but Alix was only too willing to give her the benefit of the doubt. They found dozens of horse-chestnuts among the leaves underfoot, and Alix suggested that they collect some and she would show Melissa a game when they got back to the Hall. But at the mention of going back Melissa lost interest in the idea, and the chestnuts were abandoned for another day.

Tea was served in the library, as it had been the day before. Mrs Brandon wheeled in a trolley containing scones and cakes and wafer-thin sandwiches, and Alix poured tea for herself and Melissa. But in spite of their uneasy armistice during the outing there was hostility in the air again, and Alix wished she knew of some way to disperse it.

Feeling obliged to say something, she asked: 'Did you never go for walks with Miss Stanwick, Melissa?'

The little girl shook her head. 'No.'

Alix sighed and tried again: 'But you go riding with your father, don't you?'

'Sometimes.' Melissa shrugged and took another sandwich, obviously unable to withstand the food as she had at lunchtime after all that fresh air.

Alix felt like giving up. Yesterday's dissatisfactions seemed nothing compared to today's defeats, and she could understand why teachers sometimes lost heart. But then, she reproved herself, perhaps she was exaggerating the problem. What was one day, after all? Maybe tomorrow would be altogether different.

Makoto came to collect her charge at five o'clock, and despite Melissa's antagonism, with their departure Alix was made fully aware of her own uneasy captivity. With darkness and the drawing of curtains, the pattern of her days outlined by Oliver Morgan that morning assumed a frightening unreality. She had never dreamed that he might propose to isolate her from outside influences; but then she had seen nothing particularly confidential about cataloguing a library. She had guessed he would have some reason for shutting himself away in the wilds of Northumbria, but her brief had been to find out what it was, not to become, unwillingly, a part of it. What would Willie think if he didn't hear from her soon? What would her family think? But then her mother thought she was taking up some post in Scotland on a temporary basis, and she had stressed the fact that she might not have time to contact her immediately.

The wind, which had gusted gently about the house all day, was rising as Alix dressed for dinner, and she listened to its eerie howling with a sense of hysteria stirring her stomach. She was not prone to panic unnecessarily, but right now she was close to it. Perhaps Oliver Morgan was right. Perhaps she was missing the company of men—of anyone, for that matter. Anyone, that was, who neither baited her nor insulted her, nor went persistently out of their way to be obstructive with her.

She ate alone, and retired to her room straight after. At least the television was excessively normal, and her stretched nerves relaxed a little. But as she lay in bed later, she couldn't help wishing that her employer was more accessible, and that he hadn't made it so galling for her to seek his advice.

The following morning her fears of the night before seemed foolish. The sun was shining, glinting on the frosted blades of grass, silvering the network of spiders' webs between, and daylight performed its own miracle of reassurance. Alix went down to breakfast determined not to let them defeat her, father or daughter, and not even Myra's sullen expression could dampen her mood. She half wondered if Oliver would put in an appearance, but he didn't, and she guessed that he had no intention of inviting anything that might interfere with his mood. It was a momentary setback, but she refused to let it daunt her. She would deal with Melissa in her own way, and hopefully the child would begin to show some interest in something.

The fire in the library was welcoming, and she warmed her fingers before going to the table and setting out the books ready for lessons. She had decided to try something new today. Instead of the spelling episode which had been so disastrous the day before, she would ask Melissa to compose a short story, using certain words, and that way she would also demonstrate her ability for creative writing. It might not work, of course; Melissa was nobody's fool. But she was only eight, and Alix refused to give in to an underlying feeling of inadequacy. She had been so intent on choosing the words she would use for the exercise that she was unaware of the passing of time until a knocking at the door brought her head up sharply.

'Come in, Melissa!' she called, wondering why the child should choose to knock today when she hadn't the day before, and then sighed in exasperation when the door remained firmly closed.

Guessing that this was some new ploy to annoy her, Alix got to her feet, crossed the room in a couple of strides, and wrenched open the door. She was in danger of breaking her own vow not to chastise the child, but she fell back a pace when she found Makoto outside. At once her eyes went beyond the Japanese woman to the curve of the stairs, but there was no sign of Melissa. Only Mrs Brandon was in sight, dusting the banisters, her head twisted inquisitively in their direction.

Makoto spoke, and Alix's attention was caught by what she was saying: 'My Missy not well, Thornton *san*,' she declared apologetically, shaking her head. 'Makoto says stay in bed today.'

Only then did Alix's eyes seek the face of her wrist-watch. It was almost half past nine, and she had been unaware of it. 'What's wrong with her, Makoto?' she asked now, and she knew there was little sympathy in her voice.

'Missy not well, Thornton *san*,' repeated Makoto firmly.

'So you say.' Alix was too frustrated to be tactful. 'Why isn't she well? Has she got a cold? Is she sick?'

Makoto's face seldom showed any emotion, and this was no exception. 'There will be no lessons today, Thornton *san*,' she insisted.

Alix's sigh was an outward sign of the turmoil inside her. 'Where is she?' she demanded, but Makoto just gave her a small bow and walked away. She had delivered her message, and so far as she was concerned that was that. But it wasn't.

Throwing her pen on to the table, Alix went after her, passing her easily and reaching Melissa's door long before Makoto, confined as she was by the narrow skirt of her kimono. Without bothering to knock, she flung open the door and walked in, only a little less confidently when she saw the mound of Melissa's form beneath the bedclothes. The realisation that she actually was in bed deterred her a little, but she had to go through with it now. She strode to the side of the bed and looked down suspiciously at the pale face on the pillows, but Melissa's eyes were closed, and if she wasn't asleep she was giving a good imitation of it.

Footsteps behind her heralded Makoto's indignant arrival and she tugged at the sleeve of Alix's shirt, pulling her away from the bed. With both forefingers raised she made a negative gesture with her hands, and Alix felt an impatience out of all proportion to the situation.

'What's wrong with her?' she insisted, refusing to

be appeased by Makoto's dramatics, and the little Japanese woman finally waved her arms in defeat.

'See,' she indicated, gesturing towards Melissa's head, and guessing what she meant, Alix laid her hand on the little girl's forehead. It was quite hot, and she withdrew her fingers quickly, looking resignedly at Makoto.

'Has she a chill?' she asked flatly, and Makoto shrugged in typically Eastern fashion.

'My Missy not used to getting feet wet,' she averred, and Alix gasped.

'When did she get her feet wet?' she demanded.

'Walking yesterday,' Makoto answered, her hands resuming their normal position within her sleeves. 'Missy's shoes not suit English weather.'

'Oh, for heaven's sake!' Alix couldn't suppress the exclamation. 'Hasn't she any boots? Any Wellingtons?'

'What is Welling tons?' asked Makoto, frowning, but Alix merely shook her head and walked towards the door.

'Will you tell Mr Morgan, or shall I?' she inquired, grasping the handle with all the pent-up strength of her frustration, but Makoto shook her head.

'No need to trouble Morgan. I take care of Missy. Better soon.'

Alix sighed. 'Are you sure? Don't you think she ought to see a doctor?'

Makoto bowed. It was her way of telling Alix that so far as she was concerned the conversation was at an end. Alix hesitated, tempted to insist on getting a second opinion, but then she changed her mind. If it were only a cold, Melissa would be up and about again in a couple of days. If she went running to Oliver Morgan just because his daughter had a cold, he would think her even less capable than he already did.

Nevertheless the cessation of the barely-begun lessons left Alix with more time on her hands, and she chafed against the restrictions placed on her. Could any reasonable person be expected to exist in this state of limbo? How long before Oliver Morgan considered her trustworthy enough to make a trip into the village on her own? If she could just reach a public telephone, she could ring the office and explain to Willie that things were not going to be as straightforward as he had expected. He would understand—so long as he heard something. She need not go into details. They could come later. At the moment, she didn't stop to analyse her reasons for withholding information.

It rained in the afternoon, which curtailed her plans of going for a walk, and in the evening after her solitary dinner she retired to her room again to watch television. But the following afternoon it was fine, and as Makoto had vetoed any chance of lessons that day, Alix decided to put a plan she had had into operation.

She dressed in slim navy cords and a chunky white sweater, putting on a navy anorak instead of her sheepskin coat. She didn't want to draw attention to herself, and instead of telling Seth she was going out, she let herself out of the heavy door singlehanded.

Outside the air was crisp and sharp, with the smell

of frost to quicken her step had she needed it. But the knowledge that the wolfhounds were about somewhere was more than sufficient to send her scurrying across the grass towards the belt of trees that shielded the stables. A boy was in the stable yard, grooming one of the horses, and he looked up in surprise when Alix appeared.

'Putting on her most charming smile, Alix approached him casually. 'Hello,' she said, 'I'm Alix Thornton, Melissa's governess. What's your name?'

'Thomas, miss.' The boy straightened politely, and Alix saw that he was as tall as she was. 'Can I help you?'

Alix nodded, her hands thrust into the pockets of her anorak. 'I hope so. I—er—Mr Morgan said I might borrow one of the horses. Is there a mount I could use?'

Thomas looked doubtful. 'Mr Morgan said nothing about it to me, miss. Which horse did he say you could ride?'

'Oh, he didn't.' Alix smiled again, inspiring confidence if not feeling it. 'I expect he thought you would know best. I should tell you—it's years since I did any riding, so I shan't want anything too frisky.'

The boy still looked uncertain, and determinedly she moved towards the stalls where a glossy dark head was extended. The animal shifted restlessly at her approach, and Thomas hurriedly left what he was doing to interpose himself between her and the horse.

Alix frowned and he said hastily: 'I shouldn't come too near Poseidon, miss. He's an unpredictable beast, and not at all suitable for you.'

Alix halted immediately. She had a great respect for horses, and had no wish to be bitten because of an idiotic urge to prove herself. 'What is suitable for me, then?' she queried, and was relieved to see that temporarily at least, Thomas had accepted her story. And after all, why not? Oliver had said she could ride—albeit with himself and Melissa.

Thomas opened another door and brought out a chestnut mare. Smaller than the bold-eyed Poseidon, the mare had sturdy legs and a broad back, and Alix guessed was a much older animal.

'This is Cinnamon,' he said, and Alix came forward to stroke the silky muzzle. 'You shouldn't have any trouble with her.'

'I'm sure I shan't.' Alix was charmed as the mare's gentle nose nuzzled her palm. 'She's beautiful, isn't she? Is this Melissa's horse?'

'No, miss, Miss Melissa rides her own pony. Mr Morgan bought it specially for her. Cinnamon used to be Mrs Morgan's horse.'

'Oh!' Alix was taken aback. She opened her mouth to ask whether perhaps Mr Morgan might object to her riding his dead wife's mare, and then closed it again. If she started casting doubts into Thomas's mind now, he might well decide that he needed permission from his employer before providing her with a horse at all, and that would spoil everything. So instead she hid her real feelings, and waited with no small degree of impatience for him to saddle the beast. There was always the chance that Oliver Morgan himself might appear on the scene, and she had no wish to suffer that embarrassment.

Ten minutes later she cantered away across the sloping parkland, heading in what she hoped was the general direction of the boundary fence. If it hadn't been for the uneasiness she felt whenever she contemplated Oliver Morgan's reactions to what she planned to do, she would have enjoyed the ride, but she tried, without a lot of success, to assure herself that there was no reason why he should ever find out.

Cinnamon's pace was steady, and in spite of the lapse of time since she was last on a horse, Alix felt quite at home in the saddle. Her ears stung and she wished she had had the forethought to put on a headscarf, but apart from that the actual feat of riding required no effort whatsoever.

She saw no sign of the dogs, and her hopes were rising when she came in sight of the high fence bounding the property. At first she hoped its height was a temporary thing, signifying some particular section of the boundary, but after galloping beside it for some distance she had to accept that Oliver Morgan had meant what he said when he told her she could not stray off his property.

She reined in the mare, and pulling her head round looked back the way she had come. Faint spirals of mist wreathed and curled from the damp leaves where Cinnamon's hooves had rested, but apart from that she might have been alone in the landscape. Anger and resentment seethed inside her. There was no other way out of Darkwater than the gates beside the lodge, and she might as well accept the fact.

Cinnamon nodded her head, as if in silent agreement with her thoughts, and Alix patted her neck reassuringly. 'I guess we have to go back, old girl,' she murmured, shivering involuntarily, as if the idea of riding a dead woman's horse in this lonely place invited thoughts of another kind. Digging her heels into Cinnamon's sides, she impelled her forward again, deciding that the sooner she got back to the limited kind of normality to be found at Darkwater Hall, the better.

But, curiously, Cinnamon began to play up. When Alix tried to urge her back the way they had come the mare showed no inclination to obey her, and instead sidled round until they were facing in the opposite direction.

'Cinnamon!' exclaimed Alix impatiently, trying not to show alarm. 'Come along, girl! This way!'

Cinnamon whinnied and shook her head, putting up a good show of disagreement, and when Alix again dug in her heels, she set off at a trot through the trees, taking her unwilling rider over ground she had not yet explored. Alix sighed, looking back over her shoulder at the way they should have taken, and prayed that wherever Cinnamon was headed, she would find her way back to the house before nightfall. She didn't consider dismounting. They were quite a distance from the house already, and at least on horseback she had a better chance of finding her bearings.

They seemed to go for miles, although Alix guessed her methods of deduction were as dubious as her control over the horse, but presently Cinnamon entered a wood where pine needles crunched under her hooves, and Alix had to duck her head to avoid low-hanging branches and twigs that snatched painfully at her hair.

'This isn't the way home, Cinnamon!' she exclaimed, realising that she needed the sound of her own voice to reassure her. But the memory of what Oliver had said about Darkwater Pool was invading the forefront of her mind. What if the mare was making for the pool? What if she couldn't persuade her to take her back to the house?

Then suddenly they emerged from the wood on a sweep of hillside where the grassy sward was shadowed by the dark walls of a stone-built tower. Jutting up towards the deepening gold of the late afternoon sky, it evoked all that was pagan and mysterious in this lonely landscape, and Alix shivered again, aware of her own frailty in the face of a building which had stood for hundreds of years. Looking at its stark isolation, she could almost sense the apprehension of the families who must have gathered for safety within its walls, awaiting attack or burning or worse. Horses and cattle would be gathered in the lower courtyard, and above, men and women and children would huddle together for warmth, the smoke from their fires mingling with the pungent scents of the animals. She gazed in amazement at the smoke rising from a tall chimney, and in her ears was the drumming of hooves as a reiver band came on a marauding raid. . .

The sudden panting breath of a hard-ridden animal and lean fingers reaching for Cinnamon's reins, set the mare plunging nervously, and Alix, bemused by her vivid imagination, was unable to hold on. It was all over in a moment, and she was scrambling up from the turf when Oliver Morgan dismounted and confronted her. In his dark attire, his dark face flushed with exertion, he was not unlike a reiver himself, and his first words were not intended to relieve that impression. 'What do you think you're doing?'

Alix, still trembling from reaction, was indignant. 'Don't you think I should be asking you that question?' she exclaimed, brushing damp moss from her sleeves.

'Who gave you permission to ride Cinnamon?' he snapped, ignoring her protest, and she had the grace to colour.

'I did,' she declared, sniffing. 'Why? You yourself said I should take up riding again.'

'Not alone,' he returned coldly, viewing her uneasy defiance contemptuously. 'Are you aware that you were heading in the opposite direction from the house?'

'Of—of course.' Alix continued brushing down her hips and thighs, anything to avoid his scornful gaze. 'Cinnamon refused to go back.'

'Really?' Oliver snorted. 'What an admission!'

'Well, I have admitted it, haven't I?' she gulped, unable to go on tidying herself indefinitely.

Oliver rescued Cinnamon's rein and handed it to her, his eyes narrowed speculatively. 'You weren't spying on me, then?'

'Spying on—*you*?' Nothing had been further from her thoughts, but suddenly her eyes went to the smoking chimney of the peel tower, and they widened in comprehension. 'You mean that—that's the North Tower?'

'You didn't know?'

He was sceptical, but she shook her head vehemently. 'No. If I had, I shouldn't have been so—well, I didn't know, that's all.'

'What were you about to say?'

'It doesn't matter.'

Oliver's lips thinned. 'I think it does.'

Alix sighed, playing nervously with the mare's reins. 'I was lost. If I'd known you were—well, here—I should have felt less alarmed.'

'Indeed?' Oliver's lips twisted mockingly. 'You've never given me the impression that you felt secure in my company before.'

Alix bent her head. 'Needs must. . .'

'. . .when the devil drives, I know.' He paused, looking at her strangely. 'As you're here, would you care to see my—humble abode?'

Alix quivered. 'I—I should like that,' she said, but as she accompanied him on foot across the spongy turf, she felt more than ever like the fly that was enmeshed by the plausibility of the spider.

CHAPTER SIX

THEY tethered the horses outside the tower. A narrow door was set into the stone wall, and Oliver unlocked this and went inside to switch on lights before inviting Alix to join him. She did so gingerly, stepping across the threshold into a huge barnlike area, made eerie by the canvas-shrouded blocks of stone and marble that stood like human monoliths between wooden crates and tins of varnish and other paraphernalia. In the centre of the area, lifting tackle was erected that disappeared through a hole in the floor above, and Oliver closed the door behind them and led the way towards a curving stone staircase which ran round the outer wall of the building and gave access to the upper floor.

Alix followed him nervously, reluctantly aware of what a fascinating feature this place would make; and yet curiously unwilling to contemplate making it public knowledge. It wasn't just her fear of the man himself, although in all honesty she could not be unaware of his unpredictability and of how easy it would be for someone to disappear around here and never be seen again. This tower they were in now, for instance: as they reached the upper floor, she could see the gaping hole in the middle of the floor where the tackle was erected, and guessed that a fall through on to the stone floor beneath would break every bone in her body. But more than ever she was becoming intrigued by this man, and occasionally she found herself wishing she was not here under false pretences. Of course Willie would have something to say about that, but right now his opinion didn't seem too important.

The upper floor was different from the lower one. Here there was daylight, albeit weakening now as the afternoon waned, coming through two long windows which had been let into the stone wall on the north side of the building. That explained why Alix had not noticed them from the ground; they were on the other side of the tower, and they admitted a maximum amount of light into this unusual studio. There was an unfinished sculpture on a plinth, casually covered by a muslin cloth, and the tools of his profession were strewn about the working area. But as well as these indications of his occupation there was also a narrow bed, unmade as yet, a small cooking stove, and an open fireplace where a dying log fire gave off an inadequate supply of warmth. There was also a steady humming sound, which Oliver briefly explained was a small electric generator.

Oliver let her look around for a few minutes without speaking, standing squarely before the windows so that his face was in shadow, and then he said sharply: 'Well? Disappointed?'

Alix's eyes turned from a small camp table on which reposed a half-eaten loaf, some cheese and an empty bottle of wine, and shrugged awkwardly. 'It's not what I expected,' she admitted, glancing about her. 'Why do you work here and not at the house?'

He moved so that she could see the wryness of his expression. 'Can you imagine what it would be like, working at the house?' he inquired. 'Apart from the noise I make, do you think Melissa wouldn't want to come and see what I was doing every five minutes?'

Alix shook her head. 'But this is so—so—'

'Primitive? Yes, I know. But I like it.'

'But you must be cold here!' she protested. 'Shouldn't you at least come back to the house to sleep?'

His eyes narrowed mockingly. 'Why should that matter to you?'

Alix pressed her hands down into the pockets of her jacket. 'It doesn't, of course. I—I was just stating facts. . .'

'I see. I thought for a minute. . .' His smile was sardonic. 'But no matter.'

Alix resented being made the brunt of his twisted sense of humour. 'Where you sleep matters as little to you as it does to me!' she stated hotly. 'And I should be obliged if you wouldn't imply otherwise!'

Dark eyebrows quirked. 'That was said with great feeling! Did I imply that? I didn't think so.'

'You're always implying things,' she retorted recklessly, 'and probably not only to me!'

He frowned then, and she realised she had said too much. 'Explain that remark!'

Alix backed off, coming up against the flimsy table. 'It's getting dark,' she said. 'I ought to be going back to the house.'

He came towards her, and her heart almost stopped beating, but he halted beside the plinth and flicked the muslin sheet aside, studying the roughly-formed marble beneath. 'What do you know about sculpture?' he asked, startling her.

'Not—not a lot,' she stammered. 'Mr Morgan, I—'

'For instance,' he went on, almost as if she hadn't spoken, 'do you know that there are two types—statuary and relief? Statuary being sculpture in the round, so to speak, and relief work being projected from the surface?'

Alix measured the distance from where she stood to the stairway. There was no guarantee, of course, that Cinnamon would take her back to the house, but her instincts were telling her that she had to get out of here right now.

'Have you ever been to Italy, Mrs Thornton?' he was going on. 'No? But you have heard of Michelangelo, of course. He showed that a block of marble could express emotions and feelings just as surely as any painting—that an inanimate slab of stone could be made into a thing of warmth and beauty, that could be touched as well as admired. That's the real secret of sculpture, Mrs Thornton, the ability to mould. . .and touch. . .and feel. . .'

Alix's breathing was as unsteady as the rest of her. The things he was saying, the words he was using, were as double-edged as a rapier, and just as dangerous.

'I want to go back to the house, Mr Morgan,' she blurted out childishly, and at last he gave her his undivided attention.

'Why? You were in no hurry before.'

Alix made a futile gesture. 'I'm interrupting you. . .'

He shook his head. 'No, you're not. I'd gone back to the house. That was how I found you were missing.'

'Oh!'

Alix was momentarily speechless, but when he left the plinth to approach the fire and kick carelessly at the smouldering logs with his booted foot, she moved away from the table in the hope of putting some distance between them. She had the choice of stumbling over the tools and lifting tackle, which she guessed he used to swing the huge blocks of stone from the floor below, then edging past the plinth and circling the central well to reach the stairs, or she could simply walk past him, the way she had come in. And what was she afraid of, after all? He wouldn't touch her!

Holding her head up high, she walked round his bed—and came up against the hard length of him as he stepped into her path. She gulped as the impact knocked the breath out of her, and then trembled violently when his hands linked themselves loosely about her throat.

'Tell me what you meant,' he demanded softly, and she couldn't think for the pounding of her heart in her ears.

'Wh—what do you mean?' she faltered.

'What have I implied? And to whom?'

'Oh!' She went weak and would have swayed against him had she not exercised an extreme effort of will power. 'You—you don't have to take everything I say literally.'

'But I do,' he insisted, his eyes glowing maliciously. His thumbs caressed her ear lobes. 'I mean to know. One way or the other.'

'I think you ought to let me go,' she declared unsteadily. 'I didn't ask to come here, and this—this isn't the usual way to treat a—a governess.'

'I agree. But you're no usual governess, are you, Mrs Thornton?'

'Aren't I?' she echoed. Then she remembered: 'No—no, of course I'm not. I'm a librarian. I suppose that's what you meant.'

'What else could I mean?' he countered, and she trembled beneath his probing fingers.

'Please,' she begged, 'stop teasing me!'

'Was I doing that?' he parried, and she lifted her hands in protest to push him away.

But he had loosened his thick suede jacket, and when her hands encountered the smoothness of his shirt they lingered sensuously, feeling the muscle under the silk material. As if taking her hesitation as an invitation, his hands left her throat to unzip her anorak, so that it fell open to reveal the rounded curves of her breasts, clearly outlined beneath the woollen sweater.

Immediately Alix came to her senses and would have drawn back, but his hands at her elbows prevented her, propelling her towards him. She had never been so close to a man's body before, and the hard muscle of his legs against hers robbed her of all strength.

'I imagine Myra and her mother believe our relationship to be an—intimate one, don't they?' he demanded roughly, and she could only nod her head. 'And you think I encouraged that belief?'

'I didn't say that,' she protested, dragging her face back from his chest to look up at him. 'Please—let me go!'

But the slightly cruel face looking down into hers held no sympathy for her appeal, and his dark eyes explored every inch of flushed skin and cheekbone, lingering disturbingly on the wide fullness of her mouth.

'I don't think you really mean that,' he said at last, and she twisted against him desperately, realising that the longer he held her like this, the weaker her desire to escape was becoming.

'I do!' she cried, and as she did so she became aware of a hardening in him, a throbbing urgency that spread from his body to hers and suffused her limbs with a burning heat that ran through her veins like wildfire.

'Keep still!' he muttered thickly, and she knew that he was no longer in control of the situation. And while she rejoiced in it, she also knew that this was her last chance to get away from him. If he bent his head. . .if he laid his mouth on hers. . .

But with an exclamation he set her free and turned away from her abruptly, raking unsteady hands through his hair, striving for composure. This was her opportunity, but strangely she didn't want to go. She stood there, feeling like a schoolgirl wringing her hands, and said foolishly: 'Are you all right?'

He turned on her then: 'Oh, yes. Yes, I'm fine!' he snarled angrily. 'What are you waiting for? I thought you were eager to get away?'

Alix licked her lips. 'Are—are you coming?'

'Why?' Oliver gave her a smouldering look. 'Can't you find your way back?'

Alix didn't answer him, turning away and noticing the unmade bed once more. Without really understanding why, she moved towards it, taking the blankets and pulling them straight, smoothing the covering quilt with unnecessary care.

'Leave it!' he snapped coldly, taking off his coat. Then: 'Just give Cinnamon her head. She knows the way back.'

Alix straightened. 'Of course. She was your wife's horse.'

'What's that supposed to mean?'

Alix shrugged. 'Just that. . .well. . .'

'You think Joanne came frequently here to watch her husband working?' he demanded.

'She—she must have done.'

'No!' He spoke harshly. 'Oh, she came here frequently all right—but not when I was working.'

'No?' Alix was confused.

'No.' He glared at her grimly. 'Would you like the facts? Would you like to hear how my wife spent her time when I was elsewhere?'

'No!' Now Alix looked away, staring down at the toes of her boots, realising that unwittingly she had aroused memories of a less than pleasant nature.

'Why not?' In an instant Oliver had covered the floor between them, and was standing staring down at her with tormented eyes. 'You stirred up this hornets' nest! You with your talk of things implied and never spoken; your *innocence*—that isn't innocence at all!'

'I don't know what you mean,' she declared nervously.

'But you're married yourself, aren't you?' he mocked. 'You must know what goes on. Why else are you here, and your husband almost three hundred miles away?'

Alix's face burned. 'That. . .that's different. . .'

'How? A civilised affair, is that what you mean? A mutual decision to lead separate lives?'

'Something like that.'

He stared at her angrily for a few moments, and then his face suddenly relaxed. He smiled, but his smile was crooked, and there was little amusement in it. 'Oh, Alix!' he said, and she was too distraught to notice he had used her Christian name. 'I don't believe you.'

'That—that's your prerogative, of course.'

'My prerogative,' he mimicked her. 'What long words you use, Grandmother!'

Alix took a sideways step to get past him, but again he prevented her, grasping the collar of her anorak, so that when she struggled wildly to free herself she only succeeded by leaving it in his hands. She stood staring at him impotently, her arms wrapped almost protectively around her body, and he tipped his head on to one side.

'You're not leaving without your coat, are you?' he taunted.

Alix sighed. 'May I have it, please?'

He nodded. 'If you come and get it.'

Alix came forward slowly, aware of a feeling of inevitability. She held out her hand, but he tossed the anorak aside, and caught her wrist instead, jerking her towards him.

'You—you liar!' she gasped, trying unsuccessfully to free herself, but he shook his head as he pushed her down on the bed and imprisoned her body with the weight of his own.

'You asked if you could have it,' he told her harshly, 'and I agreed. I don't recall exactly stating what.'

'Oh, you—you pig!' she choked, twisting herself desperately from side to side, but he hauled her close against his now fully-aroused muscles and sinews, and her limbs melted beneath his thrusting masculinity. When one hand imprisoned her face long enough to cover her mouth with his own, all resistance went out of her, and she yielded to the insidious desire to respond to his undoubted experience.

She sank down into the pliant softness of the mattress, her mouth opening beneath his, admitting his passionate exploration of its sweetness. Her hands, which had been trapped by her sides, slid up over his thighs and the base of his spine to lock together in the small of his back, holding him closer as his lips pillaged the hollow of her eyes and ears, his teeth fastening on her lobe and tugging her awareness. His tongue blazed its own trail of fire down her neck to where the neckline of her sweater created an impassable barrier, and she heard his muffled oath.

'Let me take it off,' he demanded roughly, and

then his hands were beneath the sweater, forcing it upward. When his mouth took possession of one hardening nipple, she moaned with pleasure, moving sinuously against him, until he said hoarsely: 'Wait!' and rolled on to his back to unfasten the belt of his pants, pulling his shirt free and loosening the buttons to reveal a brown chest lightly covered with dark hair. Alix turned on her side, watching him, half-bemused, her emotions roused to such a pitch that she was unwilling for him to move away from her. When his shirt was unfastened, she shifted so that she was looking down at him, deliberately lowering herself against him until his hand came behind her head, forcing her mouth to his once more.

He rolled over then, and his breath filled her mouth as he groaned urgently: 'Let me love you, Alix,' and buried his face between her breasts.

The sudden crash of the door downstairs as it banged back against the wall of the tower was a terrifying sound in the darkening room and even Oliver started up from the bed as a masculine voice echoed hollowly up to them:

'You up there, Mr Morgan?'

It was Giles, and with a muffled curse, Oliver rose to his feet, searching for his shirt. 'Yes!' he called tersely. 'What do you want?'

In an agony of embarrassment, Alix scrambled off the other side of the bed, pulled on her sweater and ran combing hands through her tumbled hair. She was shaking, as much from reaction as anything, but a sense of horror was filling her at the realisation of what had almost happened. Dear God, he thought she was a married woman, a woman moreover who was separated from her husband and therefore not averse to taking a lover, while she. . .she. . .

Oliver had moved to the head of the stairs, and she heard Giles explaining: 'Lady Morgan's here, sir. She arrived about half an hour ago, and nobody knew where you were—'

Lady Morgan! Alix quivered. Oh, God, what was she doing here? What would she think when she discovered her son-in-law and the governess she had supplied for him were out together?

'I'd taken Poseidon,' Oliver stated grimly, clearly not enchanted by this news, and Giles hastened on:

'I see that, sir. But you didn't tell Thomas where were going—'

'He wasn't there.'

'He'd be having his tea-break sir, like as not. Mrs Brandon gives him tea in the kitchen on cold days—'

'I'm not really interested in what Mrs Brandon does,' replied Oliver with freezing candour. 'You must have noticed there were two horses tethered outside.'

'Yes, sir.' Giles sounded subdued.

'But you chose to come in anyway.'

'The young lady's with you, sir?'

'Obviously.'

'Yes—well, young Thomas was worried about her, too. Seeing as it was getting dark, and her not used to riding here. . .'

'She's quite safe, I assure you.'

The cold irony in Oliver's voice did not go unnoticed. Alix heard Giles give a deep sigh, and then he said: 'That's all right, then, isn't it?' He paused. 'Sorry to have troubled you, sir.'

Oliver said nothing, but he flashed a look in Alix's direction and when he saw she was dressed again, the coldness of his expression almost froze her where she stood. The sound of the outer door closing with rather less ferocity signified Giles' departure, and buckling his belt Oliver walked slowly back to where she was standing. His dark face was taut with displeasure, and he reached wordlessly for his jacket and put it on.

'I suppose you want to go back now,' he stated flatly.

Alix cleared her throat. 'As—as you have a guest waiting for you, I think that would be best, don't you?'

Oliver gave her a hard look. 'Reprieve?'

'I don't know what you mean.'

'You do, you know.' He stepped aside and gestured to her to precede him towards the stairs. 'Perhaps it's just as well. I can do without that kind of entanglement.'

Alix gasped. 'You flatter yourself!'

His expression was wry. 'Don't go coy on me again, Alix. We both knew what we were doing a few minutes ago. I understand how you feel—having been married myself.'

Alix stared at his sardonic face for a moment, tempted to strike him for his deliberate provocation, but then she walked straight past him, not trusting herself to say anything more. And what could she say, after all? How could she explain to him that she had never allowed any man to touch her as he had touched her, or that the intimate aspects of such a relationship were as yet unfamiliar to her?

During the ride back to Darkwater Hall an uneasy silence prevailed, and Alix left Oliver at the stables to explain the situation to Thomas, and ran swiftly back to the house.

To her astonishment she heard Melissa's excited voice as soon as she entered the hall, and the sound of the front door closing brought both the child and the woman with her to the door of the drawing room where they had been sitting.

Lady Morgan viewed Alix's appearance with evident disappointment, as indeed did Melissa. Obviously, they had hoped to see Oliver, and after a brief word of greeting, Alix explained that he was at the stables and would be in shortly.

'You've been riding with Daddy!' exclaimed Melissa accusingly. 'And you didn't take me! You mean thing! I—I hate you!'

'Melissa!' Lady Morgan spoke reprovingly, offering an apologetic smile and Alix was at once made aware of the charm which exuded from all the Morgans. As well as being Oliver's mother-in-law, she was also his aunt, and although her dark hair was now liberally streaked with grey, she was still an extremely good-looking woman. Unlike the archetypal image of a dowager lady, she wore a slim-fitting green trouser suit, and although the pearls around her neck were real, the matching rings on her fingers were of a much more modern design. 'Melissa,' she said again, 'apologise at once!'

Melissa pursed her lips, and perhaps it was just as well that Oliver chose that moment to come in. A confrontation with the child was the last thing Alix needed just now after the events of the last hour, and besides, if Melissa were well enough to get up and greet her grandmother, perhaps she was well enough to take up lessons again. *Lessons!* Deep inside her, Alix could feel hysterically hollow laughter rising. How could she think of lessons after the traumatic emotions Oliver had aroused in her? Her sanest course would be to pack her bags and leave tonight, and forget all about the Morgans, if she could. . .

Now Oliver's cold glance flicked her like the blade of a knife before he came forward to greet his aunt, kissing her cheek with a gentleness Alix had never experienced. He touched Melissa's cheek with careless fingers, and then said sardonically: 'Well, well—my two favourite females! To what do I owe the honour?'

Alix registered the snub as she went towards the stairs, but Lady Morgan turned from greeting her nephew to say: 'Won't you join us for tea, Mrs Thornton?'

'Thank you, but no,' refused Alix politely, avoiding Oliver's cold eyes. 'I—er—I'm feeling rather tired. If you don't mind, I'll join you later.'

'Very well.' Lady Morgan made an understanding gesture, and shooed Melissa before her back into the drawing room. But as Alix fled up the stairs she was aware of a tall figure standing watching her with unmistakable impatience.

After reaching the comparative security of her

room, Alix went into the bathroom and turned on the taps. She poured bath salts liberally into the water, needing the physical sensation of cleansing they gave, sponging vigorously at her breasts, as if to erase the sensuous brush of Oliver's lips.

Afterwards, wrapped in a warm towelling robe, she curled up in a chair before her television set to try to dismiss thoughts of the afternoon from her mind. But they wouldn't be dislodged. Time and again she relived those moments in his arms, moments when all the moral teachings of her girlhood had been thrust aside by the purely sexual assault he had made on her senses. She had never felt that kind of weakness before, never thought herself the kind of girl to experience actual physical desire for a man. She thought of all the other men she had gone out with, danced and dined with, and later shared embraces with. She had all the normal reactions to members of the opposite sex, but always she had been in control—until now.

CHAPTER SEVEN

DINNER was not the ordeal Alix had expected.

After hesitating for some while over what she should wear, she had eventually descended the stairs in a simple jersey caftan, its muted shades of blue and green throwing her fair beauty into stark relief.

She found Lady Morgan alone in the drawing room, seated at the piano, running her fingers lightly over the keys, but she looked up with a smile at Alix's entrance and immediately rose to her feet.

'No, please. . .' Alix didn't want to interrupt her. 'Go on. What was that you were playing as I came in?'

The older woman glanced down at the keys. 'The nocturne?' she asked, shaking her head. 'One of Chopin's easier compositions. But I'm no pianist, Mrs Thornton. This is Oliver's piano. Haven't you heard him play?'

'No.' There was only the faintest hesitation before Alix answered, and then Lady Morgan was moving across to a drinks trolley to examine the bottles before asking the younger girl what she would like. 'Er—sherry, please,' Alix replied, more easily. 'This is a beautiful room, isn't it?'

'Yes.' Lady Morgan spoke thoughtfully, pouring sherry into two glasses and then handing her one. 'Oliver bought it furnished, of course, but the piano and one or two other articles were installed later.'

Alix's tongue explored her upper lip. 'I—I should imagine it was quite a—surprise to you when your daughter—when she and her husband decided to buy a place up here,' she murmured, hoping it didn't sound too probing.

But Lady Morgan was apparently not averse to discussing such things. 'Oh, Joanne had nothing to do with it,' she declared, indicating that Alix should sit down on one of the velvet-cushioned chairs. 'Oliver bought this place without her knowledge, and when she found out she was rather put out about it. Then. . .' She paused. 'Then she found it rather pleasant up here, and started using the place herself. When Oliver wasn't here, of course.'

Alix wondered why she said 'of course'. The marriage had been known to be precarious, but it was Oliver who had been accused of caring too little.

Taking the seat opposite her, Lady Morgan gave her a faint smile. 'Now tell me: how are you and Melissa getting along?'

Alix crossed her legs. 'We aren't,' she said honestly. 'At least, not so's you'd notice.'

'Oh!' Lady Morgan's smile disappeared. 'I had hoped—did Oliver explain what he wanted you to do? I hope you didn't object to that little subterfuge we arranged, but Oliver has to be so careful. . .' She shook her head. 'It isn't that that's causing the problem, is it?'

'Oh, no.' Alix made a negative gesture. 'I—well, I agreed to stay on and—and do what I could, but—Melissa doesn't seem to like work.'

'And have you told Oliver?'

Alix hesitated. 'Not exactly.'

'Why not?'

Alix sighed. 'Your—that is—Mr Morgan has been working.'

Lady Morgan sighed. 'You mean he's been spending his time at the old peel tower, I suppose.'

Alix bent her head. 'Yes.'

Lady Morgan sipped her sherry rather absently. 'I see. I ought to have guessed, of course. That terrible old place. Have you seen it, Mrs Thornton?'

'I—call me Alix, do,' exclaimed Alix quickly, avoiding a direct answer, and as she turned her head towards the door, Oliver himself appeared on the threshold.

In black velvet trousers and a ruffled silk shirt, he was disturbingly attractive; his attire as suitable to the nineteenth as to the twentieth century. The fine cloth stretched across his shoulders emphasised their muscled strength, and the close-fitting pants moulded the long legs and powerful thighs. Alix couldn't suppress a momentary shiver at the remembrance that only hours before she had lain in his arms, had known the intimate pressure of his body on hers, and felt the demanding urgency of his mouth. Was he remembering it, too? As her eyes encountered his, she felt a sense of shock at the contemptuous hardness in their depths. His memories were not like hers, and he was not afraid to let her see it.

'Oliver!' Lady Morgan seemed entirely unaware of any undercurrent between her nephew and his young employee. 'We've been helping ourselves to a drink. I hope you don't mind.'

'Not at all.' He strolled lazily into the room. 'I'm sorry I was not here to offer you a drink myself, but Melissa insisted I read her a story before coming down.'

Alix looked down at her drink. So Melissa had got her father to herself at last. That would please her. But what about her lessons? Did she intend that things should go on as before, and if so had he made that plain to his daughter?

'Alix. . .' Lady Morgan's smile encompassed the girl, 'Alix tells me that Melissa refuses to work,' she commented.

'I didn't say that exactly—' Alix began hastily, only to be overridden by Oliver's deeper tones.

'Melissa has been ill,' he stated curtly. 'She has been unable to attend lessons for the last couple of days.'

'Oh!' Lady Morgan looked to Alix for confirmation, and realising that anything she said was likely to be suspect in Oliver's eyes, Alix decided to be honest.

'She has had a cold!' she agreed flatly, addressing her remarks to the woman, 'but before that she made no effort to learn anything. On the contrary, she deliberately wrote wrong answers to every question I gave her.'

'Really!' Lady Morgan looked askance at Oliver now. 'Did you know about this?'

'As Mrs Thornton hasn't seen fit to tell me, how could I?' Oliver's mouth drew down at the corners.

'You were never available to tell,' declared Alix now, unable to remain silent in the face of such an oblique condemnation.

'I understand you've been spending all your time at the old peel tower,' added Lady Morgan, and Alix had the satisfaction of seeing him momentarily disconcerted.

'I see that Mrs Thornton has briefed you very thoroughly in a very short time,' he observed, pouring himself a generous Scotch and swallowing half of it at a gulp. Then: 'I do have work to do, Grizelda. I thought you would appreciate that.'

Lady Morgan sighed. 'Of course I understand, darling,' she exclaimed, getting up from her chair to approach him. 'But you have to accept that Melissa can be as wilful as her mother used to be.'

Alix felt a sudden shock. Did Lady Morgan actually know the child's mother? What a curious situation, when a man's mother-in-law could talk so casually of her son-in-law's mistress!

She looked up and encountered Oliver's eyes upon her. His face displayed the twisted cynicism she had come to know, and she looked away again as he said: 'I don't deny that Melissa isn't the easiest child to deal with, but she does have a good brain if she can be persuaded to use it.'

'I blame Makoto,' decided Lady Morgan severely. 'I don't agree with the way she fusses over Melissa—giving the child a feeling of importance which is entirely misplaced. Melissa is eight years old, and I think it's time she began behaving like other children.'

Mrs Brandon arrived to tell them that dinner was served, and the discussion was shelved for the duration of the meal. The housekeeper had excelled herself with the quality of the meal, and the roast duckling served with a tangy orange sauce was delicious. Alix ate little. For once her emotions had robbed her of all appetite, and in spite of the chaotic turmoil of her feelings, looking along the table at the inscrutable lord of the manor, she found the reality of that scene this afternoon less and less easy to believe.

Coffee was served in the drawing room this evening, and at Lady Morgan's request, Oliver seated himself at the piano. He displayed no false modesty at her request, but merely sat down and played with a complete lack of self-consciousness. To Alix, this was an entirely new facet of his character, but his casual mastery of the instrument was not entirely unexpected. Unlike his aunt, he played jazz mostly, his long fingers moving over the keys with unerring accuracy, his dark hair falling across his forehead and giving him an air of detached concentration.

When his hands left the keys Alix got to her feet to excuse herself, and Lady Morgan looked at her in surprise. 'You're not leaving us, my dear?'

'If you'll forgive me, I—I have had rather a long day,' she demurred.

Oliver rose from his seat at the piano. 'Yes, you have, haven't you?' he agreed, and only she knew the meaning behind those cold words. 'I'll speak to Melissa in the morning. Goodnight, Mrs Thornton.'

'Goodnight.'

Alix included Lady Morgan in her offering, and walked quickly out of the room. Nothing had been said about her leaving, and for the present she was still obliged to remain at Darkwater Hall.

There was a letter for her in the morning. The postmark was London, and although there was no indication of its source, she could tell by the handwriting that it was from Willie. Seth handed her the letter as she went down to breakfast, and she stuffed it nervously into the pocket of her black jeans, wishing she dared rush back up the stairs at once to read it. But there were voices in the dining room, and besides, the last thing she wanted was to draw attention to her mail.

Oliver and Melissa were seated together at the breakfast table, the first time this had occurred since Alix's arrival here, and she entered the room somewhat diffidently, feeling very much the intruder. They both looked up at her entrance, and she ran a nervous hand over the buttons of her matching denim shirt before seating herself in her usual position.

'Good morning,' she said, and they both responded, Oliver thoughtfully, and Melissa decidedly offhand. 'Are you feeling better today, Melissa?' she added, picking up the glass of orange juice already set before her and sipping slowly.

Melissa did not immediately say anything, but then, after a brief look at her father, she said: 'It's Saturday. Daddy says I can wait until Monday to begin lessons again.'

Alix could feel a spurt of irritation. 'That wasn't

what I asked, Melissa,' she said carefully, putting down the orange juice. 'I asked if you were feeling better.'

Myra appeared from the kitchen, and when she saw Alix at the table her lips grew sulky. 'You want bacon, too?' she demanded, and Alix glanced expressively at Oliver before shaking her head.

'Mrs Thornton will have toast and coffee, Myra,' he stated curtly. 'See to it!'

'Yes, sir.'

With an aggrieved air Myra disappeared again, and Alix returned her attention to the orange juice. If Willie wanted her back again she would go, she thought resentfully. Nothing was worth this kind of treatment. But then she looked up and found Oliver watching her, and in spite of the hardness of his gaze, all her reckless plans were nullified. And why? Because she was so afraid of what he would do when he discovered her real identity? Or because leaving here would inevitably entail telling her story to somebody, and she no longer felt she had that right. . .?

'Melissa will begin lessons in earnest on Monday morning,' Oliver said now. 'There will be no games and no evasions, and if you have any trouble you're to tell me.'

Alix caught her lower lip between her teeth. 'I'd rather not be accused of telling tales,' she asserted, looking at the child. 'If Melissa doesn't want to learn, then perhaps it would be easier if you waited until she went to school.'

Melissa's eyes widened apprehensively, and Oliver exhaled impatiently. 'I wanted to break her into this gradually,' he said, 'and you agreed to it. Just because you've had to face one or two minor setbacks—'

'Setbacks!' Alex was indignant. 'We've never made any progress!'

Oliver frowned. 'You will.'

'Will I?' Alix looked squarely at him. 'Can you guarantee that?'

'I think so,' he replied.

Melissa grimaced, and Alex felt a rising sense of frustration. What had she done wrong? Was it only the fact that she had insisted Melissa should work in the afternoons that had changed the child from a friendly little girl into an unfriendly one? It didn't seem logical.

Myra returned with a huge plate of bacon, eggs and tomatoes for Oliver, and some fresh toast for Alix. She assured herself that her employer was satisfied, and then actually smiled at Melissa. It transformed her plain features, and her voice was gentle as she asked the little girl whether she would like a boiled egg. Melissa refused, saying she only wanted toast and jam, and Alix, buttering her own toast, reflected how much pleasanter life would be if Myra treated her like that.

Myra departed again, and for a while they all concentrated on the food. In spite of his meagre appetite at dinner last evening Oliver ate quite a hearty breakfast, and as she covertly watched him, Alix was disturbed anew by the feelings he aroused in her. What was there about him that interfered with her mental processes in such a way that she was powerless to ignore him, that just sitting with him at a table like this she was intensely aware of him? She knew he wouldn't welcome her feelings, that in any case he didn't think of her in that way. But for all that she could understand his frustration when family matters baulked his creativity, and she wished she had been able to remove the problem of his daughter from his shoulders.

When the meal was over, he got abruptly to his feet and said: 'I've offered to take your grandmother into Bridleburn this morning, Melissa. Do you want to come?'

Melissa slid off her chair. 'Is *she* going?' she asked rudely, and Alix didn't need to look up to know she meant her.

'No,' she answered now, before Oliver could say anything. 'I have other things to do.'

'Other things?' Oliver's brows descended. 'What other things?'

Alix pushed back her chair and stood up. 'This and that,' she said, achieving a casual tone. 'Besides, I've not been invited.'

Melissa pursed her lips as her father said curtly: 'You wanted to leave the Hall a few days ago. Naturally, if you wish to join us—'

'I don't,' retorted Alix, aware that just by saying these things she was hurting herself in some strange incomprehensible way. 'If you'll excuse me. . .'

She left him then, uncertain what either of them thought, and ran up the stairs to her room. At least she had her letter to read, she consoled herself bitterly, realising she had just passed up her first real opportunity to contact Willie since her arrival here.

She flung herself on her stomach on the bed and tore open the envelope. Willie's distinctive scrawl covered two pages, but the letter's content was evident in the first few lines:

> 'What is going on, Alix? Why haven't we heard from you? Why haven't you phoned? I expect you to reply by return of post, or I shall consider taking action myself.'

Alix sighed, and rolled on to her back, holding the letter up so that she could read the rest of it. It was all pretty much along the same lines:

> 'You haven't written to your mother either, and she was quite concerned when I told her I hadn't heard from you.'

Trust Willie to get in touch with her mother, Alix thought cynically. Anything to shift responsibility if things got tough.

> 'How much longer do you expect to be away? How long does cataloguing a library take?'

If only he knew!

> 'Linsey's sent in a great feature about Harland Cosmetics, and she even had Mac go out there and take some pictures of Gertrude Harland. She's a clever girl, our Linsey, considering old Gert has always refused to have her photograph taken.'

Alix expelled her breath on a sigh. That little bit was Willie's psychology, put in purposefully to stir her up, to make her envious. Linsey Morris was younger than she was, and had only been working for the magazine for about eighteen months. But already she had proved herself capable of asking the most outrageous questions of a number of prominent people, and Willie was already talking of creating a regular column for her. Alix, on the other hand, had worked her way up from being a very junior reporter, anxiously suspecting that she would never achieve that kind of insensitivity to other people's feelings. That was why she had been so keen to come here—to prove herself! And look what had happened.

Willie's last words were typically insensitive:

> 'Is it at all possible to give me a brief outline of what you've learned so far? Or has the whole exercise been a complete waste of time?'

Alix finished reading, and allowed the hand holding the letter to fall on to the bed beside her. It was typical of Willie to hold a gun to her head, so to speak. Demanding a reply by return! He had no conception of the situation here.

She got up off the bed and walked to the window. Frost had gilded the trees, creating a tracery of white, and there was something incredibly beautiful about fields rimed like the sprinkling of icing on a cake. Oh, God, she thought despairingly, what would Linsey do in her position?

The answer was simple, of course. She would write

to Willie, and get Lady Morgan to post the letter for her in Bridleburn.

Alix turned back to face the room. She had some writing paper and envelopes in her suitcase. She could write to her mother as well, and reassure her that she had not disappeared off the face of the earth. But what could she say to Willie?

She was sitting at the table, chewing the end of her pen, when the bedroom door opened and Myra came into the room. She looked surprised to see Alix, and then gestured sullenly towards the bed.

'Didn't know you were here,' she mumbled. 'Came to make the bed.'

Alix made an indifferent movement with her shoulders. 'Well, as you can see, it's made,' she said, although she was almost glad of the interruption. She would have thought Myra would have gathered that she always made her own bed by now, but the girl wasn't very bright, as Oliver had said, and her mother probably made her check every day.

Myra departed again, and Alix returned to her letter. Apart from 'Dear Willie' she had written nothing else, and it was galling to admit that she felt incapable of imparting the startling information about Melissa's Japanese ancestry. She sighed. She was not the stuff of which reporters were made, and perhaps a tendering of her resignation might be in order.

Then she remembered Joanne Morgan's death and hardened her heart. Willie would say that the most villainous men in history had often been irresistibly attractive to women, and here she was, jeopardising her career just because Oliver Morgan had displayed a physical attraction towards her. An attraction, moreover, which he had swiftly rejected. Was she so immature that she couldn't see what he was doing? That by making love to her he might ensure a loyalty above and beyond the bounds of duty! Was that why he was prepared to take her to Bridleburn this morning, because he thought he had made a slave of her?

And yet last night his attitude had hardly been that of a lover. He had behaved as if he disliked her utterly, and Alix was not experienced enough to know whether that was a deliberate ploy or not.

With a feeling of resignation, she wrote:

'Sorry about the delay, but the situation isn't exactly as we expected. I can't explain now, but it's definitely going to take longer than we had anticipated. I'll let you know as soon as I have anything to report. Yours, etc. . .'

It wasn't a very satisfactory letter, she knew that, and Willie would be furious at the innuendo, but she couldn't help it. She simply could not baldly put down the facts at this stage. He would write again, she had no doubts about that, and when he did, perhaps she would know better how to handle it. It was the coward's way out, and she knew it.

Writing to her mother was easier. It wasn't difficult to concoct some story to satisfy her, and at least she had the satisfaction of knowing that because of the situation here, she was not tarnishing her mother's reputation as a librarian.

When the letters were sealed Alix went downstairs

again, looking for Lady Morgan, and was disconcerted to find Oliver waiting in the hall. In a cream suede jerkin and matching pants, he looked darkly disturbing, his hawklike features drawing into a frown when he saw the envelopes in her hand.

'Going somewhere?' he inquired.

Alix hesitated on the bottom stair. 'I was looking for Lady Morgan, actually.'

'Yes?'

'Yes.' She met his eyes defiantly, and then looked away from their too-penetrating scrutiny. 'I—where is she?'

'She'll be down directly,' he replied briefly. 'Why?'

Alix cleared her throat. 'I—well, I wanted to ask her if she'd—do something for me.'

'Post your letters?' he asked perceptively. 'Seth told me you had a letter this morning. Do you always reply by return?'

Alix hunched her shoulders. 'Not always. But I haven't written to my mother since I got here, and she was—concerned.'

'So you've written her two letters,' he remarked pointedly.

'No!' Alix glanced angrily at him. 'Really, this is ridiculous! I—I've written to my—uncle as well.'

'Your mother's brother?' His scepticism was obvious.

'No!' she declared hotly. 'My father's!' and then she realised what she had said. If he should see those two envelopes with different surnames he would know she was lying. And what was more upsetting still, her mother's name was Thornton, too, the same as hers, and she was supposed to be a married woman! Oh, lord, she thought sickly, what a tangled web!

Realising there was only one way out of the mess, she said quickly: 'As—as a matter of fact, I think I will come with you into Bridleburn, if you don't mind.'

'To post your letters?' he persisted.

Alix seethed with frustration. 'Among other things.'

'I'll post them for you,' he said, holding out his hand for the envelopes. 'There's no need for you to go.'

Alix pressed the letters to her breast. If only she had put them in her pocket before coming downstairs, instead of advertising their presence to anyone who cared to see! But then she hadn't realised their importance, or how easily she could be exposed. And now she was faced with an impossible decision: if she gave him the letters he could read the inconsistencies in her story for himself, and if she didn't. . .

With a gesture of defeat she handed the letters over, and he stuffed them carelessly into the pocket of his jerkin without even looking at the addresses written on them. Alix stared at him incredulously, and then realising how foolish she must appear, she turned back to the stairs again. A reprieve, but for how long?

'Alix!'

His voice halted her, and she turned to look at him reluctantly. 'Yes?'

'Did you tell your mother about Melissa?'

Alix's cheeks flamed. 'No!'

'I'm glad,' he said, a faint smile of satisfaction crossing his face, and contrarily she wished she had. He was so smug!

CHAPTER EIGHT

MELISSA was sitting at the table in the library when Alix entered the room on Monday morning. She had already set out her exercise books and her pencils, and although Alix suspected her motives she couldn't help admiring her unsmiling composure.

The weekend had passed surprisingly quickly, considering that Alix had lived in constant anticipation of being summoned to Oliver's study. But the summons had not come. Indeed, she had not laid eyes on him since Saturday morning when he took possession of her letters, and her conversations with Lady Morgan had only elicited the information that he was working once more.

But she had learned a little more about the Morgan family. She had learned, for instance, that Lady Morgan's husband was dead, and that Joanne had been their only child. That would account for Joanne's personal fortune, Alix hazarded. Her father had obviously left her a considerable sum. Apart from this, she heard about Joanne's childhood and adolescence, the hundred and one things a mother would remember.

Surprisingly enough, Lady Morgan could speak of her daughter's death without bitterness, and although Alix had heard it all before she listened intently when she was told how Joanne had skidded and crashed her car into a tree less than a mile from her home.

'It must have been a terrible shock!' she offered awkwardly, when Lady Morgan paused and stared rather sadly into space.

'Yes, it was.' The older woman sighed. 'But Oliver has been a tower of strength. I don't know what I'd have done without him and Melissa.'

That was Alix's opportunity to ask how long Lady Morgan had known about the child, but she couldn't do it. It sounded so blatant somehow, a deliberate statement that she knew that Melissa was not really her grandchild.

And so the moment passed, and afterwards Alix had enough to do in answering the equally personal questions Lady Morgan addressed to her. It was awful having to describe a relationship with an unknown man, and then invent some reason why that relationship had broken down. It was easiest to pretend that another woman had been involved, and feeling a ridiculous sense of guilt, Alix conceded that her 'husband' had been unfaithful to her.

Lady Morgan was very sympathetic, and that made things worse, so that Alix was incredibly relieved when the conversation moved to less personal matters.

And now it was Monday morning, and her lessons with Melissa were to begin in earnest. There was no Makoto to interfere, and she had Lady Morgan's guarantee that she would not appear to distract the child.

Deciding to return to the scheme of giving Melissa a story to write, Alix put the idea to her and suggested one or two titles gleaned from her small knowledge of the child's background.

'You could write me a story about Yoko,' she proposed lightly. 'I'd love to hear all about him and his adventures. Do you think you could do that?'

Melissa picked up her pencil. 'All right,' she said indifferently.

'Good.' Alix's spirits rose a little. 'And do you think you could use some of these words in your story?'

Melissa stared mutinously at the slip of paper Alix gave her. 'I don't know what all these words mean,' she said, after a few minutes.

Alix came to look over her shoulder. 'Then just use those you do know,' she suggested.

Melissa glanced up at her. 'How many words have I to use?'

'As many as you like,' said Alix levelly. 'Now, go ahead. I'll be preparing some arithmetic for us to do later.'

Melissa's dark head bent over the paper, and Alix resumed her seat at the opposite side of the table. But preparing a lesson of arithmetic took no time, and she found herself staring out of the window at the mist which as yet lingered over the frosty ground. A few flakes of snow had fallen the night before and they still powdered the grass, frozen crystals that brought beauty to the hard-packed ground. The windowpane was frosted around its rim, and added its own illusive frame to the picture. She had never realised winter could be so beautiful, living as she did in an area where snow was immediately turned to slush by the passage of many feet, and where warm buildings were vastly preferable to the smoke-laden atmosphere outside. Here was all the magic of a picture postcard, and already she could feel its spell.

Suddenly she became aware that Melissa had stopped writing and was watching her instead. The little girl's eyes were intent and rather thoughtful, and Alix felt embarrassment sweeping over her for no apparent reason.

'Have you finished?' she asked hurriedly, but when Melissa spoke it was not to answer her.

'Daddy invited you here, didn't he?' she said, through tight lips.

Alix swallowed convulsively. 'I—yes, of course he did.'

Melissa nodded. 'I guessed he did really. I just wanted to know.'

She picked up her pencil again, and would have continued writing, but Alix couldn't let it rest there. 'Why did you ask that, Melissa?' she probed. 'You know why I'm here, to teach you. And if your daddy hadn't told me about you, I shouldn't have known, should I?'

Melissa's chin jutted. 'I don't know.'

'Of course you do.'

'You're not a teacher,' Melissa insisted, 'not really.'

Alix frowned. 'Who told you that?'

'It doesn't matter.' Melissa hunched her shoulders. 'But you're not, are you?'

Alix sighed. 'No—'

'You see!'

'You don't understand, Melissa.'

Melissa shrugged her thin shoulders. 'I don't have to, do I?' she asked, unconsciously practical, and Alix wondered who had put such thoughts into her head.

She decided she would have to clear the air before she and Melissa could achieve any real understanding, and searching carefully for the right words, she said: 'Your daddy is a famous man, Melissa. You know that. And everything he does, people want to know about it.'

'What has that got to do with anything?'

'Well. . .' Alix twisted her pen between her fingers. 'If he had advertised for a governess for you, there would have been lots of newspaper men wanting to know why.'

'Why?'

Alix baulked. Why indeed? Biting her lip, she said: 'As I told you, everything your daddy does gets into the newspapers, and if they found out that he had a little girl, they would want to know all about you, and take pictures of you, and make life very unpleasant for a time.'

Melissa pursed her lips. 'I don't want anybody taking pictures of me,' she asserted, glancing self-consciously down at her lameness.

'No, well—you can't always stop it,' explained Alix, dryly, aware of her own duplicity in all this.

Melissa's brows were drawn together. 'So Daddy asked you to come and teach me?'

Alix nodded. 'Well, something like that,' she agreed uncomfortably.

Melissa stared at her for a long moment. 'Why

don't you live with your own husband?' she asked at last, and Alix felt an awful sense of inadequacy in the face of the child's frank curiosity.

'I—we—we don't get on,' she ventured at last.

'Why not?' Melissa was determined to know. 'Is it because of Daddy?'

Alix gasped. 'No!'

'Is that why Mummy was so unhappy? Because she knew that Daddy wanted you?'

'*No!*' Alix stared at her now. 'Good heavens, Melissa, where did you get all this?' Then a thought struck her forcibly. 'Was it from Mrs Brandon? Or Myra? Have they been talking to you?'

Melissa's pale cheeks flushed with colour. 'Of course not,' she declared haughtily.

Alix frowned. 'Makoto, then,' she averred. 'It has to be one or the other of them. You couldn't possibly have made this up on your own.'

'It's not made up!' cried Melissa, throwing down her pencil and getting off her chair. 'Daddy brought you here, you said so. And I know he always does what you tell him to do! He has time for you, but since you came here he never has time for me!'

Alix was on her feet too, now. 'That's not true, Melissa! Your father's been working. That's why I'm here! That is—now that I'm here, he can get on with what he has to do!'

'You were with him on Friday afternoon when Grandmother arrived!' stated Melissa accusingly. 'You know you were!'

Alix clenched her fists. 'I went riding and got lost. Your father found me.'

Melissa sniffed. 'You went to the tower with him,' she declared bitterly.

'Now how do you know that?' exclaimed Alix, aware of the weakness that still enveloped her whenever she thought of that afternoon. 'Did—did your father tell you?' *Surely not!*

Melissa was silent, and with a feeling of relief Alix guessed that she had heard it from some other source. But how? And then she remembered Giles. Of course, he could have told Mrs Brandon, and Mrs Brandon would pass it on to Makoto, no doubt. Alix ought to have realised how much the little Japanese woman would resent her for taking up so much of Melissa's time, for making her position insecure. But poisoning the child's mind was a horrible thing to do, unless she really believed it. It was possible, of course. If Melissa's mother had been unhappy, it was not unreasonable to speculate on the cause, and Alix was a convenient scapegoat. More than convenient, she thought, wondering whether she was being blamed for the breakdown of Oliver's marriage as well. But that couldn't be true, not if his Japanese mistress was still alive. Still, she could hardly say that to the child.

Now she said quietly: 'I think someone has been trying to cause trouble, Melissa. Your father and I never met until I came here to look after you.'

Melissa looked up at her suspiciously. 'I don't believe you.'

'Why not?'

'Because. . .'

'Because what?' Alix was half impatient. 'Melissa, this is silly! If you won't tell me what—'

'You don't sleep in your own bed,' declared the little girl tremulously. 'You sleep in *Daddy's*—when he's here!'

Alix sat down rather suddenly on the edge of her chair. '*What?*' she asked faintly.

'You sleep with my daddy!' repeated Melissa, tears overspilling her lashes. 'Myra told Makoto. Is he going to marry you?'

Alix could only shake her head incredulously. So this was what Melissa had been nurturing! This was why she had become so difficult, maybe even been the cause of her fever; not the wet feet as Makoto had insisted.

Now Alix pulled herself together with difficulty, and getting to her feet again, she faced the little girl. 'Makoto and Myra are wrong,' she stated steadily. 'I have never slept in your daddy's bed.'

Melissa still looked disbelieving, and Alix spread her hands helplessly. 'Why did they say I did? How do they know?'

Melissa sniffed. 'Some nights your bed isn't slept in. Myra has to make the beds, and sometimes yours hasn't been used.'

'My God!' Alix raised her eyes heavenward. 'Melissa, I make my own bed. I always have.'

Melissa bent her head. 'You would say that.'

'Aren't I allowed to defend myself?' Alix passed a trembling hand across her forehead. 'How can I convince you? You either believe me or you believe them. I can't prove it, one way or the other.'

Melissa hesitated. 'I could ask Daddy,' she said in a subdued voice.

Alix felt a cold shiver slide down her spine. 'You could,' she agreed without enthusiasm, 'but I don't think he would like it any more than I do.'

Melissa hunched her shoulders. 'Do you really make your own bed?' she asked grudgingly.

'Yes, I really do,' replied Alix, heaving a deep breath. 'And you should, too. You'll have to when you go to school.'

Melissa looked up at her through her lashes. 'Will I?'

'Yes. Everybody makes their own bed.'

'I don't know how.'

'Then I'll teach you that as well,' said Alix quietly.

Melissa bit her lip. 'You really don't sleep with Daddy?'

'I really don't.'

'But you like him?'

Alix was cautious. 'Yes.'

'He likes you,' declared Melissa suddenly.

Alix shuffled the books on the table. 'Don't you think we ought to get on?' she asked, catching the child's eyes on her. 'We've wasted an awful lot of time.'

Melissa slid back on to her chair. 'I'll tell Makoto what you said,' she averred solemnly, picking up her pencil, and although Alix was tempted to discourage her, she knew that by doing so she could undo all the good she had done. So she kept silent, and hoped that Makoto would consider that she had got off lightly in the circumstances.

Lady Morgan joined them for lunch, and she was obviously pleasantly surprised at the change in the atmosphere between Alix and her granddaughter. Melissa looked happier and more confident, and although at times during the morning she had shown signs of dissension, there had been none of her earlier sullenness. Alix herself felt as if an intolerable burden had been lifted from her shoulders, and only when she considered how impossible Melissa would make it for any girl to entertain hopes of marrying her father did a certain despondency cloud her thoughts.

When Melissa disappeared on a visit to the bathroom, Lady Morgan leant confidently towards Alix. 'Am I mistaken, or has Melissa made friends with you at last?' she whispered.

Alix forced a smile. 'I think we understand one another now, Lady Morgan,' she answered quietly.

'I'm so glad,' Lady Morgan nodded. 'I know how frustrated you must have felt. But Melissa isn't all bad. She's just reacting to an unusual amount of attention.'

Alix smiled again, avoiding a direct answer, and Melissa's return brought an end to their confidences. But at least the task she had been brought here to do no longer seemed an impossible one.

It was several days before Alix saw Oliver again, and during that time she felt she had made real progress with Melissa. The child was no longer on her guard with her, and while she had not quite resumed her initial friendliness towards Alix, she had abandoned any trace of hostility. What words had passed between her and Makoto, Alix did not know, but as she saw practically nothing of the little Japanese woman now that didn't seem to matter.

With the removal of one anxiety, however, another took its place. The fact that Oliver had made no effort to speak to her about the correspondence led her to believe that he had not been troubled to read the addresses on the envelopes, and while this was a relief, there was still the problem of what to do when Willie wrote again, as no doubt he would. She was in a quandary, made no easier by a growing awareness that she was impatient to see Oliver again and disturbingly depressed when the days passed and she did not do so. It was no use telling herself that she was just one among many so far as he was concerned. She found herself listening for the Landrover, and starting every time the front door was opened. She ached to see him with an almost physical pain, and nothing he had done could alter the feelings he had so carelessly aroused.

On Friday evening, Alix and Lady Morgan were taking coffee together in the drawing room when he suddenly appeared, unshaven and haggard-eyed, his clothes filmed with dust. He stood leaning against the door frame, uncaring that his boots were coated with the mud which had followed a sudden thaw in the weather, a faintly selfderisive smile lifting the corners of his mouth.

'It's finished,' he stated flatly, and his mother-in-law rose excitedly to her feet, her hands clasped together.

'Oh, Oliver!' she exclaimed. 'How marvellous! You must be exhausted!'

He straightened, raking back his hair with a weary

hand. 'I am pretty tired,' he agreed, flexing his shoulder muscles. 'Is everything all right here?'

His dark eyes flickered over Alix, who sat nervously by the fire, as he said this, and she answered awkwardly: 'Everything's fine, Mr Morgan. Melissa's working very hard.'

'Good.' He continued to look at her for another disruptive minute, and then switched his attention to the older woman. 'Sorry to have neglected you, Grizelda. I'll take you all out tomorrow, I promise.'

'Tomorrow you should rest,' declared Lady Morgan reprovingly. 'When was the last time you ate? Or slept?'

Oliver shook his head. 'When I'm working, I don't need food,' he said. 'As for sleeping, it gets damned cold up there when the fire goes out.'

'I can imagine.' His aunt made an impatient sound. 'Now, do you want a meal? I'm sure Mrs Brandon can rustle something up while you're taking a bath.'

'Thank you for those kind words,' he mocked cynically. 'I gather from that that I'm not fit company at the moment.' He grimaced at her discomfort. 'Don't look so upset—I was only teasing. But no, I don't want a proper meal right now, Grizelda, I don't think I could stomach it. A sandwich would be very nice, though, and I'll take a bath as you suggested.'

'Oliver!' Lady Morgan sighed her frustration. Then: 'I'll have Myra fetch you a tray.'

'No, don't do that.' His eyes turned back to Alix once more. 'I want to have a few words with Mrs Thornton. She can bring the sandwich up to my room, can't she?'

'Well. . .'

Lady Morgan looked vaguely disapproving, but Alix, opening her mouth to protest, closed it again as she encountered his hard stare. She had nothing to fear from him. He didn't even like her.

'That's settled, then,' he said, turning away. 'Give me fifteen minutes, Mrs Thornton, then you can come up.'

His aunt looked at him thoughtfully. 'Will you be coming downstairs again, Oliver?' she asked, and he shook his head.

'I thought not, if you'll forgive me. As you said, I'm tired.'

Lady Morgan's eyes softened. 'That's right, you get a good night's sleep, Oliver. I'll see you in the morning.'

He nodded and smiled, and without looking at Alix again left them.

After he had gone, Lady Morgan rang the bell for Mrs Brandon, and when that lady appeared, explained that Mr Morgan was back and would like a sandwich.

'Yes, my lady.' Mrs Brandon was always polite to her employer's relatives. 'I'll send it up to his rooms, shall I?'

Lady Morgan glanced quickly at Alix. 'Er—no. Bring it here, Mrs Brandon. Mr Morgan will be coming down for it.'

'Yes, my lady.'

The housekeeper departed and Lady Morgan raised her eyebrows at Alix's surprised stare. 'Servants talk,' she stated, without dissembling. 'We don't want that, do we?' Alix shook her head, and she went on: 'Oliver's used to that sort of thing, you're not. He should know better than to expose you to it.'

Alix got jerkily to her feet. 'Lady Morgan, I hope you don't think—'

'I don't think anything, Alix. I just know you're a very attractive young woman, and a sensible one too, I hope. With one unsatisfactory marriage behind you, I imagine, you would think very seriously before becoming emotionally involved again.'

Alix inhaled deeply. Lady Morgan was quietly letting her know that she shouldn't take anything Oliver said or did too seriously. And if she thought it necessary to warn her, she must think the warning was warranted. But why? Was she so transparent? Had Lady Morgan noticed her obsessive interest in the comings and goings at the Hall, or sensed her restlessness throughout those long evenings when Oliver had not appeared? It was humiliating to think that anyone might have suspected something which she had thought was successfully disguised.

'Lady Morgan—' she began, but the older woman had resumed her seat on the other side of the fireplace and now held up her hand repressively.

'There's no need to say anything, my dear. What either you or Oliver do is no concern of mine, I know that. I just wanted to make sure you understood.'

Alix turned away, running moist palms down the sides of her maroon velvet pants. Were all divorced or separated women subjected to these oblique comments regarding their relationships with men? Why was it assumed that because a woman had been married she would welcome any man's attentions?

Women were not like men. They didn't need a constant assuagement of the senses, and Lady Morgan, as a widow herself, should know that!

Mrs Brandon returned with a tray on which reposed a plate of sandwiches under a persplex cover, and a jug of strongly-flavoured coffee. She glanced speculatively at Alix, still standing beside her chair, as she placed the tray on the low table beside Lady Morgan and accepted her thanks with an ingratiating smile. Then she departed again, leaving Alix to face the daunting task of delivering the tray.

'You'll come down again?'

Lady Morgan was speaking and Alix gathered her thoughts. 'What? Oh, yes. Yes.' Then she spread her hands. 'I don't even know where his room is!'

'No?' Lady Morgan's lips tightened. 'Well, Oliver's suite is partly above this room. If you turn left at the head of the stairs, it's the last door at this end of the gallery.'

Alix absorbed this, and with a feeling of apprehension bent to pick up the tray. If any of the staff saw her her reputation would be in shreds, and had it not been for Lady Morgan's presence, she would have told him about Melissa's accusations. Surely then he would have thought twice before insisting she played maid.

In spite of the hall and stairs stretching out like a marathon course before her, she made the landing without incident, and walked quickly along to the door at the end of the gallery. She knocked lightly on the panels, deciding she wouldn't give him a second chance if he didn't hear her the first time. Lady

Morgan could come and tell him his sandwiches were waiting for him downstairs, and that would solve the problem.

But contrary to her expectations, he did hear her, and the door opened almost at once. She didn't know what she had expected—a bath towel perhaps, draped carelessly about his hips, or silk pyjamas which would reveal far more than they concealed of his lean indolent body. Certainly not clean but faded denim jeans and a matching denim shirt, buttoned almost up to the neck. He was clean-shaven now, and only his hair, still damp from the shower and shining beneath the artificial lights, revealed that he had stripped and dressed again.

'Come in,' he said, stepping aside so that she could enter the room, and she carried the tray into a comfortable, if slightly austere, sitting room. Apart from a honey-coloured carpet on the floor, there was a plain brown leather suite, a small writing bureau, and a couple of reading lamps illuminating well-filled bookshelves. The curtains were brown and cream, and matched the shades on the lamps, but there was none of the ostentatious luxury to be found downstairs.

He closed the door and took the tray from her, carrying it across to a low table set between the armchairs. Then, ignoring the coffe's appetising aroma, he straightened and said: 'What's the matter? Did you think I'd planned a big seduction scene?'

His words were so close to what she had been thinking that Alix found herself denying them hotly, insisting that her only concern was why he wanted to see her.

Oliver frowned, and gestured to one of the chairs. 'Sit down, won't you? I wanted to talk to you about Melissa, and in the morning I might not get the chance.'

Alix subsided on to the couch to avoid the intimacy of facing him across the coffee cups, although her blood had cooled considerably since his mocking accusation. She ought to have known that Melissa always came first with him, and not allowed Lady Morgan's insinuations to influence her in any way.

Oliver remained standing, however, towering over her so that her eyes were on a level with his hips, and she had to force herself not to stare at the carved buckle of his belt.

Now he said, 'You said downstairs that the child is working well. Is that true? Has she stopped being awkward?'

Alix nodded. 'Yes. She's been very good really.'

'And Makoto? You've had no trouble with her either?'

'No.' Alix shook her head.

Oliver digested this silently for a few moments, and then he said: 'I wonder why she chose to be so disobedient last week. I thought, in the beginning, that she liked you.'

Alix pressed her palms together. 'So did I,' she murmured uneasily.

Oliver inserted his thumbs into the back of his belt, arching his spine as if it ached. 'And you've no idea why she played you up?'

Alix bent her head. 'Does it matter?'

'Yes, I think it does. I don't like to think that she's capable of taking an unreasoning dislike to anyone.' He sighed. 'She's been too much in the company of older people. Perhaps because Makoto was upset over the change of arrangements, she was being loyal to her.'

'Yes.' Alix felt uncomfortable, but she was finding it impossible to tell him the truth, particularly after what he had just said. He might think she was making it up. After all, he must be used to girls making a play for him. With a wife and a mistress in his past, he was not inexperienced in the ways of women.

'What do you think?' he asked now, and she wished for once that she had a little of Linsey Morris's cheek. She wouldn't hesitate, Alix was sure. She would tell him straight out that his daughter had thought she was his mistress!

When she didn't immediately answer, he lowered himself on to the couch beside her, his weight causing her to slide a little way towards the middle. She put her hands down on the edge of the couch to prevent herself from slipping any nearer to him, and he moved so that his thigh imprisoned her fingers. She looked up at him aghast, her cheeks flushed, and tugged her hand free.

'If. . .if that's all. . .' she began nervously, her voice trailing away as he caught her fingers again, caressing her palm with his lips before pressing her hand against his chest.

'I didn't come straight home this evening,' he told her softly as his eyes moved disturbingly over her, coming to rest briefly on the laced neckline of the velvet jerkin which matched her pants. 'I went down to the Lodge to see Giles. . .and he told me a story.'

'He did?' Alix didn't see where this was leading, and her main concern was to get away from him, away from the intimate pressure of his leg against hers.

'Yes,' Oliver was saying now. 'I didn't believe it at first, but now I'm not so sure. It's a tale that's circulating about you. . .and me.'

'A-about you and me?' echoed Alix falteringly.

'That's what I said,' he averred, his breath warm against her cheek. 'And I think you've heard it, too.'

'I—have?'

'I believe so,' he asserted definitely, and looking down, he deliberately unfastened his shirt so that her fingers were resting against his still damp flesh. Then he looked into her eyes again. 'Wasn't that a rather provocative thing to do?'

Alix gasped. 'You think that I—*oh*!' Her heart pounded indignantly. 'I certainly didn't suggest such a thing!'

'You didn't?' Hooded lids narrowed his eyes. 'Then who did?'

His calculated cynicism caught her on the raw, and with an angry exclamation she dug her nails hard into his chest so that he uttered a violent oath and released her instantly. As she sprang to her feet, she saw in horror that blood was spurting from four distinct scratches, trickling down his chest and staining the blue denim of his shirt.

Her momentary alarm at what she had done, however, gave him the advantage, and with a savage '*Come here*!' he caught her wrist and jerked her down beside him again.

Uncaring that his blood would stain her jerkin too, he forced her back against the yielding upholstery, and covered her parted lips with his own. Alix tried to fight him off, but the hungry pressure of his mouth released all the pent-up longing inside her, and with a little moan she wound her arms around his neck and gave herself up to the pulsating ecstasy of his kiss. He kissed her many times, long devouring kisses that sapped her strength and left her weak with longing for him.

'So you didn't tell anyone about what happened at the tower?' he muttered, as he released her lips to bury his face in the hollow between her breasts.

'No,' she protested, looking at him through half-closed lids, and with a groan he sought her mouth again.

He was trembling, one leg imprisoning both of hers, when he raised himself slightly to look down at her. 'So who did?' he persisted. 'Grizelda?'

'No.' Alix stretched out her hand to touch the blood on his chest, smearing it between her fingers. 'Giles must have told Mrs Brandon that I was with you, and she—she probably told him that we—slept together.'

'What?' Oliver stared incredulously down at her.

'It's true,' she said softly, raising her fingers to her lips and touching them delicately with her tongue. 'Just because I make my own bed—'

'Oh, *God*!' he groaned, crushing her mouth

beneath his. 'I want to sleep with you, Alix, and I don't much care whose bed we use.'

Alix responded to him urgently for a few seconds, and then, when he pushed her jerkin aside and bent to kiss the smooth skin of her midriff, she managed to say the words which she knew he had to hear: 'Oliver—Melissa thought we slept together, too.'

There was a moment when his tongue continued its sensuous trail to the hollow of her navel, and then suddenly he was still, and his hands gripping her hips hardened.

'What did you say?' he demanded harshly, lifting his head.

Alix was terribly loath to repeat what she had said. Lying here in Oliver's arms, she was where she most wanted to be, and right now she was uncaring of the consequences. But he had to know, and in normal circumstances she doubted she would have dared to tell him.

She licked her lips, and said quietly, 'Melissa—Makoto heard gossip in the kitchen, and—well, I suppose she felt justified in telling her.'

Oliver swore, and pushed himself up until he was kneeling beside her. 'You mean Makoto told Melissa that you and I—oh, God! How could she?'

Alix trembled. 'That—that was why Melissa was so awkward with me. Because—because she was jealous, I suppose.'

'*Jealous*!' Oliver said the word contemptuously, getting up from the couch to pace restlessly about the room. 'My God, save me from jealous women!'

Alix pulled her jerkin down over the waistband of

CHAPTER NINE

ALIX didn't sleep well, and she came downstairs on Saturday morning feeling dull and heavy. The fact that it was a foggy morning, too, did nothing to lighten her mood, and she wondered apprehensively if there would be another letter from Willie to complete her depression. It was a week since she had given her letters to Oliver to post, and she had half expected that Willie would reply by return, too, leaving her in no doubt as to his feelings. But there had been no word, and it crossed her mind fleetingly that Oliver might not have posted the letters at all.

When she entered the dining room, it was to find Lady Morgan and Melissa already seated at the breakfast table, and the little girl looked up immediately and said: 'Daddy's finished working, and he's going to take us to Newcastle today!' in excited tones.

Alix took her seat. 'Lucky you!' she said, giving Lady Morgan a faint smile. 'But isn't it foggy this morning?'

'It will probably clear before lunchtime,' remarked the older woman, offering Alix the coffee pot. 'You look rather tired, Alix. Are you feeling well?'

Alix busied herself with the coffee cups. The previous evening when she had rejoined Lady Morgan in the drawing room, she had been the recipient of a series of contemplative glances, and it seemed that a night's sleep had in no way diminished the older woman's curiosity. But, as on the previous evening, Alix merely admitted to a slight headache and made no attempt to satisfy the questions underlying her words.

Melissa, noticing nothing amiss, went on, 'Daddy came to my room this morning and told me we were going to Newcastle,' she declared boastfully. 'Grandmother thought he might be tired after working so hard, but he said it was time we did some Christmas shopping. Do you know, it's only three weeks to Christmas?'

Alix hadn't known, actually, although now as the child had said it she realised that December had come in unannounced, and that she had been at Darkwater Hall for over two weeks. Two weeks! She made an effort to shake the depression from her. So much had happened in such a short space of time, it was difficult to believe that it was only two weeks.

Myra was fetching more toast when Oliver appeared. In a navy corded suit and light grey shirt, he looked more formally dressed than Alix had seen him, and she wondered if this was his professional image, cool and detached, hooded lids revealing none of his inner feelings.

'Daddy!' Melissa slid off her chair to approach him, her limp hardly noticeable to Alix now, she was so used to seeing it. 'Are you ready to go?'

'Just about,' he agreed, and Lady Morgan exclaimed, 'But you haven't had any breakfast!'

'I had it earlier,' he explained, meeting Alix's gaze before she hastily looked away, 'in the kitchen. Some people might say I was more at home in there.'

'Whatever do you mean?' Lady Morgan's eyebrows arched. 'Oliver! I don't like that kind of talk. Now, we're still going, I gather, in spite of the fog.'

'I know the road, Grizelda,' he remarked curtly, much to Melissa's evident relief, and then turned back to Alix. 'Will you come with us, Mrs Thornton?'

Alix looked up at him in confusion. 'I—oh, no, I don't think so.'

'Why not? Do you have anything better to do?'

There was an edge to his voice which she didn't understand, and she was half relieved when Lady Morgan said mildly: 'It is Alix's day off, you know, Oliver!' and Melissa added that perhaps Mrs Thornton had something better to do, herself a little put out by his concern for the governess.

Alix could sense Oliver's rising impatience, but not the cause of it. With a feeling of helplessness, she exclaimed, 'I've got a headache, actually, Mr Morgan, and I don't think trailing around shops will improve it, do you?'

He thrust his hands into the pockets of his trousers, and as he did so his jacket opened so that she could see, between the buttons of his shirt, the faint outline of an elastic plaster. Immediately, the vivid remembrance of what that plaster covered came back to her, and her eyes went to his face as if searching for a similar reaction. But he was wearing a curiously defeated expression, and her heart seemed to stop and then start again with erratic rapidity. It was crazy, because he entertained nothing but contempt for her, but at that moment she could have denied him nothing.

'It's possible that you need some air,' he replied flatly. 'But if you'd rather stay here. . .'

'All right, I'll come!' she cried, aware that by obeying him she was displeasing both Melissa and her grandmother, but unable to retract the words now. 'But I'm not ready.'

'We can wait,' Oliver responded calmly, and with a gesture of impotence she left the room.

It was going to be cold, and Alix dressed warmly, in a midi-length skirt that hid the tops of her suede boots, and her sheepskin coat. She had a matching hat and scarf and she put those on, too, winding the long scarf around her neck so that the ends trailed almost to the hem of her skirt.

When she went downstairs again only Melissa was waiting in the hall, and she surveyed her sulkily. Praying she was not going to have more trouble with the child, Alix looked down at Melissa's feet, and said: 'Don't you have any boots at all?'

Her question disconcerted the little girl and she frowned down at her leather shoes. 'No. I had some rubber boots once, but they got too small for me, and Makoto threw them away before we left for England.'

'Then I think we'll have to get you some, don't you?'

Melissa's eyes widened. 'Could we?'

'I don't see why not.' Alix hoped she wasn't being presumptuous. But she didn't think Oliver would refuse to buy his daughter a pair of boots.

Melissa was looking infinitely brighter, and when

Lady Morgan came down the stairs, pulling on her gloves, Melissa greeted her with Alix's suggestion.

The older woman's eyes moved to Alix's face. 'Yes,' she said, 'I think that's a good idea, Melissa.' She reached the hall and patted the child's shoulder. 'Where's Daddy?'

Melissa made a gesture towards the door. 'He's gone to get the car,' she explained, a momentary shadow crossing her face again as she seemed to remember that Alix was accompanying them. Then she smiled. 'Come on—he's probably waiting for us.'

Not knowing what to expect except the Landrover, Alix was reluctantly impressed by the sleek Mercedes that awaited them outside. She had never travelled in such a vehicle, and when Oliver came round to open the door for Lady Morgan, his derisive expression revealed his awareness of her feelings. He made Alix feel uncomfortable, as if she cared about his personal possessions, and she got into the back of the car beside Lady Morgan with flushed cheeks.

Melissa had scrambled into the front without waiting for permission, and was now busily locking herself into her seat belt. She insisted that Oliver wore his too, and he humoured her before setting the powerful car in motion.

Alix had a curious feeling as they left the grounds of the Hall. She supposed it was much the same sort of feeling that the Borderers must have had, emerging from their peel towers after a siege. A sense of escape that was tinged with a certain vulnerability, as if one was loath to exchange the security of confinement for the doubtful advantages of freedom.

The drive to Newcastle was accomplished without too much difficulty. The fog was still quite thick but the roads were comparatively clear at that hour of the morning, and Oliver kept the Mercedes' speed down to a modest fifty. Any lack of conversation between the adults was made up for by Melissa's excited chatter, and apart from an awkward silence when she blurted out Alix's suggestion that she needed some boots, the journey was accomplished without incident.

Newcastle was crowded, however. Christmas shoppers thronged the streets and arcades, and although Oliver was able to park his car without difficulty in the reserved space he kept in the multi-storey car-park near Northumberland Street, it was obviously not going to be so easy to go shopping.

'I think we'd better split up,' he declared, when they emerged from the fume-laden atmosphere of the carpark, and Alix felt a momentary sense of shock. Was he going to suggest that she spent the day with him? Had he changed his mind about her, or did he simply not trust her?

She was quickly informed. 'I think Melissa ought to go with Mrs Thornton,' he said, ignoring the little girl's instant protest. 'She knows the sort of things the child needs, and it's important that Melissa should have some warm clothes for the winter.'

'But, Daddy, you said we were spending the day together!' his daughter exclaimed disappointedly. 'Why can't we all go shopping?'

'It's too much of a scrum,' he said, glancing round

at the hurrying hordes of people. 'Melly, don't be difficult. I'm not saying we can't all meet for lunch somewhere, and maybe this afternoon we can go to the Toy Fair.'

'The Toy Fair?' Melissa's lips lifted again. 'Oh, could we? Could we, Daddy?'

'If you're a good girl this morning,' agreed her father dryly. He turned to Alix. 'Do you think you could cope with buying a child's wardrobe? And some boots, as you suggested?'

Alix held up her head. 'Are those your instructions?' she inquired stiffly.

His eyes darkened with some emotion she could not identify, but there was no mistaking the hardness of the fingers that gripped her arm under cover of the pressing mass of people. '*Alix!*' he muttered, his warm breath fanning her ear. 'Don't make this any more difficult than it already is!'

Alix looked down, and forcing a smile to her lips, she deliberately stood on his toe. A grimace of pain crossed his face as he took a backward step, and bestowing a triumphant look in his direction she took Melissa's hand.

'That sounds like fun, doesn't it?' she asked the little girl, and reluctantly Melissa agreed.

She was aware that their exchange had not gone entirely unnoticed by Lady Morgan, but she couldn't help it. Oliver couldn't have it all his own way—insisting that she needed the outing, and then unloading the necessity of buying clothes for his daughter on to her shoulders. Had that been his intention all along? Had that been the reason for his determination that Alix should join them? Didn't he care that there were dozens of telephones scattered about the metropolitan area—that she had only to dial a reverse-charge call to betray his hitherto closely-guarded secret? Or was the effort not worth the candle?

Now he had recovered himself sufficiently to pull out his wallet and extract a handful of notes. He handed them to Alix, saying curtly, 'This should be enough. If it's not, pay a deposit on the things and I'll settle the balance after lunch.'

Alix took the money rather unwillingly. She didn't like the idea of Oliver giving her money. It smacked too strongly of collusion, of payment for services rendered. But she was being ridiculous, and she knew it, so she took the notes from him and stuffed them into the capacious depths of her shoulder bag.

'Right. . .' Oliver had pulled on a fur-lined jacket over his suit and now fastened the buttons determinedly. He put a hand on his aunt's shoulder and said: 'Where shall we eat? Do you want to go to an hotel, or would you like some Chinese food?'

Lady Morgan glanced over her shoulder at him. 'Oh—Chinese food, I think,' she said. 'How about you, Melissa? Do you like Chinese food?'

'Melly likes anything,' said her father abruptly, looking at Alix. 'Mrs Thornton?'

'Count me out. I'll just get a sandwich in Woolworths,' she exclaimed offhandedly, and saw the familiar impatience in the whitening of his knuckles.

'Chinese it is, then,' he said harshly, 'I'll book a

table for four. Wah Chin's at one o'clock, Mrs Thornton. Don't be late.'

In spite of Melissa's initial antagonism and her own sense of indignation, surprisingly Alix enjoyed the morning. They found a boutique in one of the larger stores that stocked exactly the kind of modern children's clothes that they were looking for, and in a short time Melissa was modelling pants suits and dresses, skirts and sweaters, and an adorable jersey coat with a pleated back that flared as she moved. She soon forgot to be self-conscious about her leg, and paraded up and down eagerly for Alix's benefit. She liked trousers best, for obvious reasons, but the dresses were so pretty, with wide sleeves to take a blouse or a sweater worn underneath. There was a leather skirt and waistcoat that fastened with braided thongs, and pretty jeans with daisies embroidered around the pockets and hems.

The sales assistant was soon enchanted by Melissa's enthusiasm, and spent more time than she should have done in ransacking the racks of small garments for every article that would fit her.

At last, after much consultation, it was decided that they would have two dresses and a pants suit, the leather two-piece, the green jersey coat, and last, but not least, the daisy-patterned jeans. Melissa had never had jeans before, and she watched the assistant intently as she folded everything into large plastic carriers.

There was just time left to go to the shoe department, and Melissa saw at once the boots she would like. They were made of red leather, and fastened with laces instead of zips, and Alix decided to add a pair of yellow gumboots to her already arm-aching load, so that Melissa should not be able to complain of wet feet after any walk they might care to take.

It was a few minutes after one when they entered the restaurant, and Melissa, skipping ahead, saw her father and grandmother at once. They were seated at a table in one of the cubicles that provided privacy all around the outer circle of the restaurant, but when Oliver saw his daughter he left his seat to come and take the plastic bags from Alix's tired hands.

'You should have left them to be collected!' he exclaimed, examining her flushed face with eyes that showed a certain impatient concern.

'I want to show you what I've got, Daddy!' cried Melissa, tugging at his arm. 'We got heaps of things!'

'Not really,' said Alix deprecatingly, looking forward to sitting down, and urged Melissa ahead of them as Oliver escorted her to the table he had reserved.

'Thank you,' he added, in an undertone, and she flashed him a helpless look before going to take the seat on the banquette next to Lady Morgan.

But Oliver, who had stowed the carriers beneath the seats, gestured that Melissa should sit beside her grandmother, and much against her better judgment Alix found herself sitting beside Oliver and opposite Lady Morgan.

Oliver took his seat beside her, and then said: 'Would you like a drink?'

Alix hesitated, and Lady Morgan, as if feeling obliged to say something, observed: 'A dry Martini is always a good aperitif, I always think.'

'Thank you, I'll have a Martini, then,' agreed Alix nervously, and Oliver nodded.

Melissa soon recovered her high spirits. Turning to her grandmother, she exclaimed: 'I've got some jeans! Just like Mrs Thornton's, except mine have got daisies on the pocket.'

Lady Morgan sipped her own Martini. 'That's not all, I hope,' she remarked dryly, and the little girl giggled.

'Oh, no! I got some dresses—and a coat—and a suit—'

'Keep your voice down, Melly,' reproved her father good-humouredly. 'Do you want the whole restaurant to think that you hadn't an item of clothing to your name until this morning?'

'No, but honestly, Daddy, we found some pretty things.'

'I'm so glad.'

'Mrs Thornton knew exactly where to go.'

'I thought she might,' murmured Oliver quietly as the waiter returned with Alix's Martini and a lemonade for Melissa. He, like his aunt, had ordered his lager earlier, and now he asked for the menu.

There was a great variety of meals to choose from, but Alix, whose throat was feeling particularly tight with the awareness of Oliver's thigh only a couple of inches away from hers on the banquette, found it difficult to think about food. She wasn't especially hungry, and she would have preferred the anonymity of a sandwich at a supermarket snack bar.

Melissa was making a great show of choosing her

lunch. It was an exciting event for her, eating in a public restaurant, and she and her grandmother pored over the menu with evident enthusiasm.

While they were doing so, Alix opened her bag and gathered the remainder of the notes to give back to Oliver. But when she showed them to him, he said softly, 'Keep them as a gift. Buy yourself something you would like.'

'No.' Alix shook her head, and thrust the notes fiercely into his hand. 'I don't need payment for shopping with Melissa,' she declared, in an angry undertone. 'Nor—nor for anything else!'

Oliver's mouth tightened, but he took the notes and pushed them carelessly into his coat pocket. 'How about your salary?' he inquired caustically, but she concentrated on the menu and wouldn't look at him again.

But his mention of her salary brought the whole aspect of her situation here back into perspective. The point was, how could she accept a salary when she was already being paid by the magazine? And how could she accept payment from the magazine when she wasn't doing the job she was being paid to do?

'What are you going to have?'

Oliver was speaking to her once more, his voice cooler than before, and she looked at him tormentedly, aware that no matter what happened her life would never be the same again. She thought of all the lies and prevarications that lay between them, manufactured for her protection, and wished, with all the power that was in her, that she dared to tell him she was not the person she claimed to be. What would be his reaction? she wondered apprehensively, remembering his uncertain temper. He would be furious, of course, but would he try and understand her position? Would he appreciate the fact that she had kept what she had learned to herself, or would he see her enforced silence as simply a lack of opportunity? And how could she prove to him that it wasn't? Unless she told him about Willie. . .

Unaware, she had been staring at him intently for several seconds, and it was fortunate that Melissa had distracted her grandmother's attention by hauling out the carrier containing her new boots for display. But Oliver was returning her stare, and what he could read in her eyes had banished some of the coldness from him.

'Well?' he said softly. 'Have you decided?'

For a minute she thought he had read her thoughts, and coloured deeply. Then she realised he was talking about the food, and looked hurriedly down at the menu again.

'I—er—chop suey would be nice,' she stammered, her voice subsiding abruptly when his fingers curved possessively over her knee.

'Alix,' he said in a tortured voice, 'I love you!'

Never could such a declaration have been made in such unsuitable surroundings, with Melissa chattering to the waiter who had arrived to take their order, and Lady Morgan complaining that she couldn't decide between the prawn salad and the chicken chow mein. Yet for a brief moment in time they were immune from the everyday sights and sounds of the restaurant, and Alix's fingers covered his with shaking urgency. His hand turned to grasp hers compellingly, and a faint smile touched the corners of his mouth as he acknowledged her surrender.

Alix felt weak as she contemplated his mouth and the disturbing awareness of how that mouth would feel against hers—against her skin—against the whole trembling length of her. But was he serious? What did those hoarsely-spoken words presage? He said he loved her—but how many other women had heard him use those same words, and why should she assume that they were anything more than an extension of the things he had said to her the night before? Love meant different things to different people, but why should he choose to say it here of all places?

'What are you having, Daddy?'

Melissa's shrill little voice distracted them, and although he retained his hold on Alix's hand under cover of the menus, Oliver managed a teasing smile for his daughter.

'Let me see,' he said, pretending to study, 'I'll have a chicken chop suey, I think. How about you, Alix?'

His unexpectedly casual use of her name did not go unnoticed and catching Lady Morgan's eyes, Alix felt wretched. Oliver's aunt was not one to hide her feelings, and what was more, the opinion she held could well be right. After all, Oliver believed Alix was a married woman, and although he said he could not afford to get involved in a divorce case, perhaps he had decided to take advantage of something that was so blatantly offered. She shivered, remembering her response to his lovemaking. Did he think she was like that with any man? That her experience of marriage had left her desperate for a substitute? And had he decided to take her up on it? But why tell her he loved her, unless he understood her so well that he guessed a declaration was the kind of thing she would respond to. . .

Now she pulled her hand free of his and said tensely: 'Chop suey, please!' before deliberately handing the menu back to the waiter.

The orders were made and Lady Morgan leant across the table towards her. 'Did you buy anything for yourself?' she asked.

Alix shook her head. 'I—no. We didn't have time.'

Oliver shifted on the banquette so that his leg was against hers, and determinedly Alix put a few more inches between them. She was aware that he gave her a curious look, but then Melissa captured his attention again and she breathed more easily.

'I expect you'll be going home for Christmas, won't you, Alix?' persisted Lady Morgan, playing with the stem of her glass. 'Will you be seeing your husband?'

If Alix had been in any doubt before, this latest gambit would have confirmed her suspicions of Oliver's aunt's intentions. But she remained calm, and answered quietly: 'No, I shan't be seeing—my husband, Lady Morgan,' ignoring the temptation to see whether she could hurt Oliver as he was hurting her.

Oliver himself pulled a case of cheroots out of his pocket, and putting one between his teeth said, 'I don't think Alix will be going home for Christmas, Grizelda. We're likely to be snowed up by then, and I don't think she should risk making the journey to London when it's possible she might not be able to get back again.'

Cool grey eyes surveyed his aunt across the table, and Lady Morgan looked down into her Martini. 'Do you think that's a good idea, Oliver?' she asked, and Alix was aware of the double meaning behind her words.

'I think Alix must decide for herself,' he replied levelly, and the older woman caught her breath.

'I probably shall go home—to my parents' home—for Christmas,' Alix interposed quickly, and knew that she was the cynosure of at least two pairs of eyes.

Before anything more could be said, however, the waiter arrived with their individual requirements, and the confusion of plates and dishes took up a considerable amount of time, so that it was easier to concentrate on the meal than attempt a compromise.

But Alix simply couldn't eat hers. Her throat had closed up completely, and in spite of swallowing several glasses of the white wine Oliver had ordered to drink with the meal, she found it impossible to get more than a few mouthfuls down. She noticed that Oliver was eating little of his either, and even Lady Morgan seemed abstracted. Only Melissa ate with enthusiasm, interspersing forkfuls with further information about her new wardrobe.

It was after two o'clock when they emerged from the restaurant, and Oliver suggested stowing the things they had already bought in the car before going on to the Toy Fair. They all agreed, although Alix would have much preferred them to leave her, so that she had some time to get her thoughts into perspective before returning to Darkwater Hall. What seemed obvious now was that somehow she had to tell Oliver the truth, and then she would know his real intentions. If he threw her out, and it seemed likely, at least the guilt with which she was burdened would no longer weigh so heavily on her. Of course there were any number of complications—like who was Melissa's mother and what did she mean to him now?—and Melissa's own feelings towards any woman who might conceivably divert her father's attentions from her. But whatever happened, she could no longer go on living a lie.

Once the carriers had been disposed of, Alix made an effort to escape. 'I do have one or two things I'd like to buy,' she murmured, 'and now that Melissa's fitted out, you don't need me any longer.'

Oliver's eyes narrowed. 'You don't want to come with us?'

'It's not that,' Alix sighed, 'I'd just like to do some shopping for myself, that's all.'

'Perhaps Alix wants to buy some personal things, Oliver,' remarked Lady Morgan mildly, but Oliver ignored her.

'You can do your shopping after we've been to the Toy Fair,' he persisted grimly. 'Can't you?'

Alix was trying to find some reason why she could not when his aunt spoke again. 'Look, Oliver,' she said, 'why don't you take Melissa to see the toys, while Alix and I go shopping together? I'm sure Melissa would love having you all to herself for once.'

There was studied reproof in her words, and while the last thing Alix wanted was a tête-à-tête with Lady Morgan, she knew she had no choice. Melissa deserved some time alone with her father.

'Yes,' she agreed now, smothering the impulse to banish the slightly hunted look from Oliver's face, 'that's all right with me.'

Oliver thrust his hands deep into his pockets, and she sensed his angry frustration. 'Very well,' he said at last, giving in to Melissa's excited pleas. 'We'll meet back here at four o'clock.'

'Make it four-thirty,' suggested his aunt, tucking her arm through Alix's. 'That will give us time to have a cup of tea before we meet you.'

Oliver inclined his head curtly, and after a brief word of farewell, he and Melissa left them, disappearing into the crowds without a backward glance.

Deciding she was not going to give Lady Morgan time to indulge in idle conversation, Alix made a determined effort to accomplish all her own Christmas shopping in the space of two hours. As well as her mother, she had a married brother and his wife and their two children to buy for, and there was a certain satisfaction to be gained from finding exactly the right gift for each of them. Her mother loved jewellery, so that was easy, and an amethyst brooch suited her very well. She bought a book on sailing for her brother, and some perfume for his wife, and spent a little longer choosing some games for the children. They were five and three, and only just beginning to take an interest in board games, and there was quite an assortment to choose from.

It crossed her mind that perhaps she ought to buy gifts for Melissa and Lady Morgan, and Oliver, as well, but she didn't really know where she would be at Christmas.

Lady Morgan began to get impatient towards four o'clock. She had bought nothing but hand cream, and she began to insinuate that she was needing a rest.

'Look!' she exclaimed, as they came into Fenwicks from Eldon Square, 'the restaurant's on the second floor. Let's go up and have a cup of tea.'

Alix was reluctant, but she realised she couldn't be selfish, and Oliver's aunt was looking a little weary now. The lift transported them to the restaurant itself, and although it was quite full the waitress managed to find them a table in a corner.

'What a relief!' Lady Morgan exclaimed, fanning herself with her handkerchief. 'I'd forgotten what it was like to trail from store to store.'

'You needn't have come,' Alix reminded her dryly, allowing the other woman to take charge of the teapot while she lay back in her chair and relaxed for the first time that day.

'Oh, yes, I need,' Lady Morgan contradicted her, when the tea was poured. 'I wanted Oliver to go with Melissa. They need to get to know one another better, those two.'

Alix let this go. She was not prepared to instigate a discussion about Oliver's merits as a father.

But of course Lady Morgan insisted on going on. 'What do you think of Melissa?' she asked intently. 'Really think of her, I mean, not just because she's your reason for being here.'

Alix sighed. 'I like her,' she replied guardedly. 'She's no better and no worse than any other little girl.'

'You don't think she's—well, a little insecure?'

Alix put down her teacup. 'What are you trying to say, Lady Morgan?'

The older woman looked shocked at this sudden reversal of their roles. 'I beg your pardon?'

Alix leant towards her. 'All this talk about Melissa! You don't really want to know what I think of Melissa. You want to know what I think of her father!'

'You don't know her father,' replied Lady Morgan quietly. 'He was a Japanese film director that Joanne met when she and Oliver went to Tokyo in 1975!'

CHAPTER TEN

To say that Alix was stunned was an understatement. Lady Morgan was actually telling her that Melissa wasn't Oliver's child at all, but that of his wife and some unknown Japanese film magnate. It was staggering.

'I knew you'd be shocked,' the older woman said now, looking at Alix's pale face. 'You thought Oliver had had a mistress, didn't you? Well, he didn't. He never has—to my knowledge, at least. Joanne was the unstable half of that marriage.'

'But—' Alix couldn't take it in. Her mind refused to function normally. 'Why—why wouldn't he acknowledge the child before his wife's death if he intended to do so afterwards?'

Lady Morgan shook her head. 'I'm afraid you don't understand, my dear. Oliver didn't know about Melissa until about eighteen months ago. Then. . .' She sighed. 'In the course of one of their arguments, Joanne threw the information at him, hoping, I suppose, that he would agree to give her grounds for a divorce.'

'Joanne wanted a divorce?'

'On her own terms,' agreed Lady Morgan, nodding. 'You see, the terms of her father's will were rather unusual. Andrew—my husband—knew what Joanne was like, and he put certain rather awkward clauses in his will to the effect that should Oliver have grounds to divorce Joanne, she would lose everything.'

'So she hoped that if Oliver learned about—about Melissa, he might decide to give her her freedom?'

'Something like that,' the older woman responded.

'But—he wouldn't?'

'No.' Lady Morgan sighed again. 'Oh, I realise you don't know Oliver as well as I do, but even you must realise that he is an honest man—a compassionate man. As soon as he learned that Joanne's daughter was hidden away in some remote Japanese island, he insisted on meeting her, and both of them flew out to Hokkaido to see the child. Of course, you can guess what happened. Melissa took to Oliver at once, and Oliver would have brought her back to England there and then had Joanne been willing.'

'She wasn't?'

'Heavens, no!' Lady Morgan was vehement. 'Could you imagine what Joanne's sophisticated friends would have to say about Melissa? For years they had been sympathising with her. She always maintained that Oliver made their life together difficult, that he was a brute and a womaniser, using her money as a stepping stone to his own success. It wasn't true, of course, but Oliver let her get away with it. I think he felt some obligation towards my late husband—it was he who promoted Oliver's exceptional talent—and maybe he thought that without him, Joanne didn't stand much chance of surviving. She was always a very highly-strung, wilful girl, a little like Melissa is now, but I wasn't blind to her weaknesses, as she thought I was.'

Alix absorbed her words with an effort. Melissa was not Oliver's child, she kept telling herself incredulously. There was no haunting Japanese beauty in the shadows of his past, and Melissa's resemblance to him was simply that of family likeness—Joanne had been his cousin, after all.

Then other thoughts invaded her mind. Lady Morgan had erased the stigma of Melissa's illegitimacy from Oliver's shoulders, that was true, but was she also aware she had provided the perfect motive why he should wish Joanne dead? At her death, he inherited a tremendous amount of money, as well as the opportunity to acknowledge Melissa as his daughter.

Thrusting these thoughts aside, however, she said, 'Why are you telling me all this, Lady Morgan?'

The older woman lifted her shoulders. 'I thought you would be interested.'

'I am. You know I am. But—'

'Look!' Lady Morgan broke in gently. 'I know how you feel about Oliver.'

'You—do?'

'Of course. Don't be like Joanne and imagine that because I'm sixty-three I've lost the ability to see—and feel. I know you're attracted to him, and perhaps he is attracted to you, but—and it's a very big but—don't be fooled into thinking that he might be serious.'

Alix couldn't let that go. Oliver had said he loved her, after all. 'Why not?' she demanded.

'Because,' Lady Morgan paused, 'although Oliver

inherited Joanne's estate when she died, if he marries again, he loses it.'

Alix's cheeks flamed. 'He might not care.'

'I think he would.'

'Why?' Alix stared at her.

'Because of Melissa, of course. Do you think it's fair that he should deprive Joanne's daughter of her mother's estate?'

Alix rested her elbows on the edge of the table, cupping her hot face in her hands. Of course, Oliver would not do that. If he had been prepared to bring Melissa to England at whatever cost to his wife, he would hardly be prepared to deny her a secure future now. And his work, no matter how successful at present, could not be said to be a steady profession.

'So you see. . .' explained Lady Morgan, 'what I'm telling you is for your own good. And in any case, aren't you forgetting something?'

'What?' Alix frowned.

'Why, your husband, naturally. And I further doubt that Oliver would expose Melissa to the publicity of a divorce case at this stage in her development.'

And Melissa herself was no small problem, thought Alix miserably. She had made it plain from the beginning that she would not welcome another woman to dilute her adopted father's affections.

Alix pushed her teacup aside, and linked cold hands together in her lap. 'So what do you think I should do?' she asked in a small voice.

Lady Morgan looked thoughtful for a moment, then she said: 'I think, when you go home for

Christmas, as indeed you must, you should not come back.'

'And—and Melissa's education?'

'We'll get someone else. Someone older, I think. I did think you were somewhat unsuitable at the time, but if you remember, I had no alternative but to choose you.'

Alix bent her head, unable to meet her eyes, sure that the reasons she had been sent here must be mirrored in hers for anyone to see. How successful she had been, she thought bitterly. In this brief space of time she had learned everything she had come here to learn, and if she wrote her story now, Willie would feel his faith in her during the past five years had been justified. And if she didn't write the story, and she had no intention of doing so, she would no doubt be fired on the spot. . .

'Heavens!' Lady Morgan was looking at her watch now. 'It's after four-thirty! Oliver and Melissa will be waiting for us. Come along, my dear, we must hurry. Oliver doesn't like to be kept waiting.'

Alix gathered her bags and parcels and followed Lady Morgan into the lift, but her movements were slow and automatic and they reached the ground floor without her being aware of it.

Outside, the older woman jostled her along, giving her occasionally anxious stares, as if, Alix thought in a moment of lucidity, she was half afraid of the consequences of her uninvited confidences.

Oliver and Melissa were waiting outside the car-park, stamping their feet to keep warm. The crowds of shoppers had thinned somewhat now, although the traffic more than made up for any lessening of activity by pedestrians. Oliver started forward as Alix and his aunt appeared, and it was obvious from his expression that he was not well pleased.

'Where the devil have you been?' he demanded, and Alix noticed he addressed his remarks to her and not to his aunt. 'It's after a quarter to five. Couldn't you have left whatever it was you had to buy until another day?'

'It was my fault, Oliver,' put in Lady Morgan soothingly. 'I insisted on having a cup of tea in Fenwicks, and by the time we were served—'

'Let's get in the car, shall we?' suggested Oliver abruptly, and Alix surprised a rather anxious expression on Melissa's face as they walked into the building. She had said nothing since they appeared, and Alix guessed that she had borne the brunt of her father's anger. Poor Melissa!

No, lucky Melissa! a small voice inside her jeered cruelly. She had been given the right to live with Oliver for as long as she liked! He had let nothing stand in the way of that.

The Mercedes was chilled after standing for several hours in the stone-built surrounds of the multi-storey car-park. Even so, it was much warmer than being outside, and Alix hoped the isolation of the journey back to the Hall would cushion her against what would come after. She still intended telling Oliver her real identity, and then it would be up to him whether she left forthwith or waited until Christmas as his aunt had decreed. Either way, she could not afford to be weak. No matter that her worst suspicions had not made any difference to her feelings for him; Melissa had had a raw deal until now. Alix couldn't deprive her of the future that was rightly hers, even supposing Oliver should ask her to, which seemed very unlikely after he learned the truth about her deception. She shivered as she contemplated his reaction to her confession. Facing Willie seemed a mild fate by comparison, and she spared little thought for what she would do after her dismissal from the magazine. *Sufficient unto the day*, she quoted silently to herself with despairing aptness.

The fog had cleared and Oliver made excellent time on the journey home. The Mercedes simply ate up the miles, and Alix guessed he was expunging some of his own frustration in an exhilarating turn of speed. Even Melissa lost her anxious expression and, turning in her seat, began to tell her grandmother all the exciting things she had seen at the Toy Fair. And she really was her granddaughter, Alix thought emotionally.

'There were dolls that could suck a feeding bottle, just like a real baby!' Melissa declared, wide-eyed. 'And then. . .' She glanced hopefully at her father. 'And then. . .they wet their nappies!' She giggled. 'Imagine that!'

Oliver made no comment, however, and it was left to Alix and Lady Morgan to show interest in what the child was saying. The little girl was clearly disappointed at her father's reaction, but she had learned not to expect more than he was prepared to give her.

In no time at all it seemed they were stopping before the tall iron gates of Darkwater Hall, and Alix wondered if the journey had seemed so short because she was dreading what must come after. Giles came out to open the gates for them, but when Oliver would have driven straight past, he put up his hand to halt him.

'Excuse me, sir,' he said, hurrying to the window that Oliver impatiently opened, 'but there's visitors at the Hall.'

'Visitors!' Alix could almost physically feel Oliver's freezing anger. 'I thought I left orders that no one, but no one—'

'I know, sir, I know.' Giles was clearly distressed. 'But—well, it's the young lady's husband, sir, and he insisted on being admitted.'

Alix's mouth opened. Her husband! But she had no husband, she wanted to cry hysterically. In God's name, what was going on?

Oliver looked round at her, and even in the paltry light cast by Giles' torch she could see the anger glittering in his eyes. 'Did you invite your husband here?' he demanded.

Alix shook her head helplessly. She couldn't tell him here, not like this, not with Lady Morgan and Melissa looking on, avid with curiosity. 'I—I don't know anything about it,' she exclaimed. That, at least, was the truth!

Oliver swung round to face Giles again. 'Very well,' he said abruptly, winding up his window, and leaving the anxious gatekeeper staring after them, he sent the Mercedes' wheels spinning as he depressed the accelerator.

Alix was first out of the car when it stopped before

the steps that led into the Hall. She looked about her frantically, searching for another vehicle, but whoever had assumed her husband's identity must have arrived on foot, as she herself had done. Oliver got out and opened the door for his aunt while Melissa helped Alix gather her parcels. They were all aware of the tenseness in the atmosphere around them and Alix thought how easily tempers could erupt.

Seth opened the door as they were unloading the boot, and he came down the steps to help carry the bags. Lady Morgan took his arm to mount the steps and Melissa ran ahead, leaving Oliver and Alix alone for a moment.

Alix looked anxiously up at the lighted doorway, and then with a feeling of desperation, she said: 'Oliver, there's so much I want to explain.'

His rejection was almost tangible. 'Isn't it a little late for that?' he inquired grimly, snapping shut the boot.

Alix sighed. 'I hope not,'

Oliver straightened, his expression bleak. 'Why aren't you hurrying in to greet your husband?' he demanded. 'Whatever you say, he must care about you to come all this way to find you.'

Alix caught his arm despairingly. 'Oliver—oh, Oliver, whoever that man is in there, he's not my husband!' She shook her head. 'I don't have a husband.'

'*What?*'

Oliver was still staring at her unbelievingly when a shadow fell across them as a man came to stand in the shaft of light issuing from the open doorway.

Alix turned her head instantly, aware of vaguely hostile eyes upon them, and then she said, 'Willie!' in a horror-stricken voice.

'Hello, Alix.' Willie came down two steps, and then looked disbelievingly over his shoulder. When he turned again, his expression was almost as accusing as Oliver's.

'What a deceitful girl you are!'

Alix stared into his unfriendly blue eyes. Why had she never noticed how closely set they were, or how pouched the skin beneath them? Willie was a big man, but his body was over-indulged and out of condition, and beside Oliver's lean frame his thickening waistline bulged unbecomingly. She knew he was younger than Oliver, only thirty-five or thirty-six, but the demands of his profession had taken their toll in more ways than one.

Now Alix knew it was up to her to say something, and mounting the steps to reach him, she said sharply: 'What are you doing here, Willie?'

Willie looked beyond her to the man who was mounting the steps behind her. Then he assumed an ingratiating expression. 'Now is that any way to treat your husband?' he chided.

Alix clenched her fists. 'You don't have to go on with that, Willie!' she told him coldly. 'Oliver knows you're not my husband—I've just told him.'

Willie's expression changed. 'Oh, have you? That's very interesting. And does he know why you're here?'

Alix's cheeks flamed. 'Not yet.'

Oliver reached them. The words that had passed

between them had carried easily to his ears, and now he said, 'I suggest we all go inside,' and waited for them to precede him into the building.

Another surprise awaited Alix in the hall. Linsey Morris was hovering anxiously by the door leading into the drawing room, her agitation dissipating somewhat when she saw Alix and Willie. Then Oliver followed them inside, closing the door behind them, and her brown eyes widened with evident anticipation. Alix had never liked the other girl. She was everything that Alix was not—small, slender as a reed, with a cap of chestnut hair that clung silkily to her well-shaped head. But Alix had never disliked her more than at the moment her greedy little eyes alighted on the man Alix knew she herself loved. . .

Willie seemed to recover his composure once he had Linsey to support him, and holding out his hand to Oliver, he said: 'As Alix seems reluctant to make introductions, sir, I'll introduce myself. My name's William Faulkner, and this is my assistant, Linsey—'

'I know who you are, Mr Faulkner,' Oliver interrupted him abruptly, walking across to the library. 'Will you come in here, please? Then we can continue our conversation without interruption.'

Willie glanced sharply at Alix, and then he and Linsey hurried after their host. Alix herself hung back. She didn't want to be a part of their conversation. She didn't want to hear Willie explaining why he had sent her here, or to see Oliver's undoubted contempt. That Willie should have presumed on her letter to gain entry to Darkwater Hall was bad enough, but that Oliver should recognise him and still be prepared to listen to what he had to say was worse, somehow. If only she could have prepared him in some way, if only she had told him the truth last night!

'Alix!' Oliver's voice broke into her thoughts, and she lifted her head to look at him.

He was standing in the doorway to the library, and she decided she could not blame Linsey for being attracted to him. She had been, after all, but it was a futile exercise for either of them.

Now she looked down at her parcels, and said: 'Do you mind if I dispose of these?'

Oliver looked over his shoulder into the library where his two uninvited guests were warming themselves before the fire. Then he strode quickly across the hall to where Alix was standing, and she fell back a step in alarm, half afraid he was going to strike her. But his voice was curiously rough, as he said impatiently: 'You look frozen! And shocked out of your mind!'

Alix licked her dry lips. 'Wouldn't you be?' she challenged tremulously.

Oliver stared at her for a long minute, and then he raked long fingers through his hair. 'I ought to break every bone in your body!' he muttered harshly.

Alix shook her head. 'I—I wanted to tell you,' she protested. 'But—'

'But you didn't!' he snapped shortly. 'Why not? Was it safer to pretend?'

'Safer?' Alix shook her head. 'Well, I—I suppose so.'

'What will you do now?'

Alix tried to think coherently. 'I—well, go back to London, I suppose.'

'I see.' Oliver's nostrils flared. 'And will you write your—story—for this magazine?'

'No!' Alix's lips trembled. 'That—that's why Willie's here now. He thinks I've let him down.'

Oliver muttered an oath and turned away. 'Go to your room,' he said shortly, 'I'll deal with this. I'll speak to you later.'

Alix wanted to protest, but she had no desire to enter into arguments with Willie in front of Oliver, culminating as she was sure they would in her dismissal. The last thing she wanted was Oliver's pity, or the ignominy of Linsey's triumph. She wanted to crawl away somewhere and hide, but Darkwater Hall possessed no hiding places.

As she was going upstairs Melissa appeared, after the library door had closed uncompromisingly behind her father. She came to stand looking anxiously up at her, and when Alix went on her way, she came after her.

'What is it?' she cried. 'What's wrong? Why are you crying?'

'I'm not crying!' exclaimed Alix, rubbing determinedly at her cheeks. 'I—your father and I had a little disagreement, that's all.'

Melissa looked unconvinced, and when Alix reached her bedroom the little girl was just behind her. 'Can I come in?' she asked, and without waiting for permission, opened the door.

Alix dropped her parcels on to a chair and turned

to survey her small visitor. 'Where's your grandmother?' she asked.

'She's rung for tea in the drawing room,' explained Melissa, frowningly scuffing at the carpet with her toe. 'She told me to keep out of the way.'

Alix couldn't prevent a half smile. 'But you didn't,' she pointed out.

'No.' Melissa hunched her shoulders. 'Why was Daddy so angry? Are you going back to London with your—husband?'

Alix sighed. 'He's not my husband, Melissa,' she said, unable to dissemble any longer. 'I'm not married.'

'You're not?' Melissa's eyes were wide. 'But why did you say you were?'

'It's a long story,' said Alix, trying to be business-like. 'Now, what did I do with my handbag?'

Melissa retrieved the bag in silence and handed it to her. Then she said thoughtfully, 'So you won't be leaving?'

Alix felt an hysterical laugh rising inside her. 'I think I probably shall,' she said tautly.

'But why?' Melissa stared at her. 'Has Daddy asked you to go? Was that why you were crying?'

'Melissa, I wasn't crying!' Alix could feel her nerves stretching ominously. 'But—well, I think your father would agree that in the circumstances it's best if I do go.'

'What circstan—circust—what do you mean?'

Alix pressed her lips together. 'Oh, Melissa! I've—I played a trick on your father. I'm not really a governess, or a librarian. I—I work for a magazine.'

'You mean—you write stories? Things like that?'

'Something like that,' Alix agreed.

'But you can teach. You've been teaching me!'

'I know, darling, but anyone with a reasonable education could do that. Teaching's not hard. Not if you have patience.'

Melissa sighed, obviously trying to absorb what Alix was saying. Then she said surprisingly: 'But I don't want you to go. I don't want anyone else to teach me. I want you.'

Alix shook her head. 'Melissa! Good heavens, at the beginning of the week you resented me being here!'

'That was before—' Melissa broke off abruptly. 'I don't believe Daddy wants you to go.'

Alix let that go. 'We'll have to see, won't we?'

The little girl regarded her anxiously. 'If Daddy asks you to stay, you will, though, won't you?'

How could she answer that? Alix could not find words to make any definite statement. Besides, even if Oliver was prepared to let her stay, she *should* leave. She didn't think she could bear to live in close proximity with him without revealing her feelings, and although she loved him she would not become his mistress. She would never take the risk of bringing another unwanted child into the world, and anything else was out of the question.

But now she said, 'I think you'd better go and have tea with your grandmother, Melissa. We'll talk about this later.'

Melissa left with evident reluctance, and Alix was warmed a little to know that at least the child's antagonism for her seemed to have disappeared. Perhaps that small experience of her father's displeasure as they waited outside the car-park that afternoon had convinced her that it was best not to depend wholly on one person. Or perhaps she was afraid her father would employ another governess, one she liked even less than Alix.

Either way, it had no real bearing on Alix's situation. She quailed at the thought of the interview which was being conducted downstairs, and dreaded the moment when she would have to face Oliver again. Knowing Willie, he would doubtless capitalise on the fact that he had gained access to Darkwater Hall, and remembering his puzzled expression when he emerged from the Hall to greet them, she guessed he must have seen Melissa too, and been struck by her resemblance to the Morgans. He would probably misjudge the child's parentage as she had done, and she felt a terrible sense of responsibility for the whole sorry affair.

If only she could get away from the Hall. If only there was some means of escape without having to face Oliver again! What was there left for them to say to one another, after all? And even if he forgave her when he discovered she had not betrayed his secret, which was by no means certain, there was still the insoluble dilemma of Melissa's inheritance. And could she really live the rest of her life with a man who she suspected of causing his wife's death?

Half-unthinkingly, she pulled her cases out of the cupboard and began packing them. Wild thoughts chased through her brain, thoughts of absconding with Oliver's car, parked so casually outside, taking the chance that Giles might not notice who was driving when he came out to open the gates. Or perhaps she could walk to the gates. Surely Giles couldn't refuse to let her out if she insisted on leaving! And then she remembered the dogs, and her stomach sank. The idea of facing them alone and unaided in the dark was a terrifying prospect indeed.

Then another thought occurred to her. No matter how Willie and Linsey had got to the Hall, someone would have to take them back to the railway station, or alternatively to catch the bus. She was sure Oliver would see that they were escorted from the premises, and as his car was there at the door. . .

She paced anxiously about her bedroom. They would not be spending the night at the Hall, that much seemed certain. Oliver would never permit it. And in any case, they had no reason for staying. Once their interview with Oliver was over they would be leaving, and while Alix had no desire to accompany them, there might be a way she could do so unseen. The boot of the Mercedes was spacious, she had seen that when Oliver stowed Melissa's wardrobe inside. It was certainly big enough for her to squeeze in and pull down the lid, just far enough for it to appear closed without actually being so. Then, while Oliver's attention was diverted by Willie and his companion, she could slip out unobserved. Or at least she could slip out. If she was observed, Oliver was unlikely to cause a scene in some public place, particularly with Willie and Linsey looking on.

The idea gathered momentum. It was more than

an idea, it was a definite possibility, but one which she would have to decide upon immediately if she was to stand a chance of succeeding. Her cases presented the biggest problem. They were too big and bulky for her to bring downstairs without attracting anyone's attention, so although she had packed them, they would have to be sent for. She could take her handbag with her, of course, and once she reached home she had other clothes to wear until Oliver was persuaded to send her belongings back.

Trembling a little, Alix zipped on her boots again, picked up her handbag and gloves and opened her bedroom door. As she came down the stairs she could still hear the low rumble of voices from the library, and she breathed a sigh of relief that so far her plan was working.

The door opened without too much effort on her part, and she could hardly believe her luck when she stepped out into the frosty night air. The door closed silently behind her, but she had to face the fact that if the boot of the Mercedes was locked, she might well find it difficult to explain why she had been outside once more if she had to go back indoors again.

The boot wasn't locked. Oliver had finished unpacking its contents while Alix had been pleading with him earlier, and he had simply closed it before following her and Willie into the Hall. With a feeling of intense apprehension, Alix lifted the lid and climbed inside, breathing a sigh of relief as the darkness closed about her. The lid dropped easily into position, and she wedged her scarf in the gap so that it could not close completely and trap her inside.

She seemed to lie there for hours before anything happened. The cramped position she was forced to maintain made her feel sick, or perhaps it was simply the awareness of what she was doing and the risks she was taking to escape from this unfunny charade that caused her stomach to react so violently. She was a coward, she acknowledged that silently in the darkness, but even cowards had some contribution to make.

At last, when she was seriously contemplating the possibility of getting out to stretch her aching body, she heard the sound of a door opening and the murmur of voices coming nearer. She breathed a sigh of relief as she recognised Willie's Irish burr, and the deeper tones she knew to be Oliver's. Then, when she was waiting in anticipation for them to get into the car, she heard the sound of another vehicle coming swiftly up the drive, and anxiety took the place of expectation. It was the Landrover, she guessed, before she heard the door slam and Giles' respectful tones, but when her spirits sank in anticipation of Giles escorting Willie and Linsey off the premises, the Mercedes door was opened, and its springs absorbed the weight of someone getting inside. She breathed another sigh of relief. Oliver must have sent for Giles to drive the Mercedes, which would certainly make things easier for her at the other end—wherever that was.

The door was slammed and the engine started, drowning all other sounds in Alix's ears. It was infinitely less agreeable riding in the boot than on the comfortable leather upholstery, and her already aching limbs protested vigorously at this unwelcome jostling. It was difficult, too, to keep the lid of the boot from flying up as the wind got inside and tried to snatch it out of her cold hands.

After only a short distance the car stopped, and Alix listened intently for some indication of why this should be so. Then she remembered the gates and breathed again. Of course, if Giles was driving the car he would have to open the gates as well.

As if to confirm this point, she heard the metallic click as the gates swung wide, and then Giles came back and drove the car through, stopping a few yards further on to close the gates again.

She waited impatiently for him to get back into the car again. Soon now she would be on her way to Bridleburn, or even Newcastle, and from there it should not be too difficult to find her own way back to London. If Willie and Linsey Morris happened to catch the same train, that was just too bad. She would face their anger when she came to it.

She sighed. Giles was taking an awful long time closing those gates, she thought anxiously. A thought struck her. Could he possibly have noticed the end of her scarf protruding from the boot? Was he even at this moment considering it, and its implications? She winced as her shoulders moved in an involuntary shrug and dug into the metal base of her hiding place. No one would notice a trailing shred of wool in the dark.

After another few moments she could bear the suspense no longer. She determined to take a look, albeit a surreptitious one. With painful caution, she managed to lever the lid slightly so that she could peer over the rim, but blackness met her horrified gaze. And not the blackness of darkness either. She was not out on the open road, but locked inside some dark prison where the only smells were those of oil and exhaust fumes. A garage, in fact.

Gasping in dismay, Alix thrust the lid wide and clambered out, uncaring that she might ladder her tights in the process, intent only on gaining escape from this horrible place. Dear God, she would be missed, she thought in agony, and how on earth would she explain her absence?

But there was worse to come. When she eventually found the doors which she had foolishly imagined were the gates to the Hall, she found they were locked, and nothing she could do would open them.

CHAPTER ELEVEN

OLIVER entered the dining room at seven-thirty that evening to find only his aunt seated at the table. His dark gaze went broodingly over the chair which Alix usually occupied, and then settled on his aunt's anticipatory features. Lady Morgan smiled, but received no answering salutation, asked, 'Have they gone?' in surprisingly tactless tones.

Oliver pushed his thumbs into the waistband of his denim pants, and rocking back on his heels, countered: 'Where's Alix?'

Lady Morgan frowned. 'Alix? But—didn't she leave with her husband?'

'William Faulkner is not her husband!' declared Oliver tersely. 'He's the editor of a magazine that isn't known for its discretion in people's private affairs! Alix isn't married.'

'What?' Lady Morgan gasped. 'You don't mean that—that she—'

'—worked for the same magazine?' Oliver's voice was bored. 'Yes, that's exactly what I mean.'

'But, Oliver. . .' His aunt was nonplussed. 'Oh, that deceitful girl! How—how could she?'

Oliver's nostrils flared. 'The point is, she didn't,' he stated flatly. 'That's why Faulkner came here.'

Lady Morgan shook her head confusedly. 'Even so, when I think of the way I confided in her. . .'

Oliver sighed. 'Save the dramatics, Grizelda. Where is she?'

'Well, how should I know?' cried his aunt, taking out her handkerchief and blowing her nose. 'I haven't spoken to her since we got back from Newcastle.'

'You haven't?'

'No.' His aunt regarded him indignantly. 'When I came indoors she was with you.'

'But didn't she have tea with you and Melly?'

'No, she did not. Melissa told me she'd gone to her room, and I assumed it was to pack. Melissa said she was thinking of leaving—'

'Melissa said *what*?' Oliver looked positively furious. 'When was this? What did Alix say?'

'Oh, what does it matter?' exclaimed his aunt impatiently. 'The girl was an impostor. I, for one, am glad to see the back of her.'

'Well, I'm not!' retorted Oliver coldly. 'And you'd better get used to that idea.'

'Whatever do you mean?' Lady Morgan looked astounded.

'I mean that if I can persuade Alix to stay, I shall.'

His aunt looked pale. 'But. . . Melissa. . .'

'What about Melissa?'

'You—you were going to adopt her.'

Oliver uttered an oath. 'What does that have to do with anything? I still intend to adopt her. Don't worry, Grizelda, I've already set the machinery in motion. Melissa shall have what is right and properly hers.'

'But—but what if Alix—'

'Leave Alix to me,' said Oliver quietly, and then

paced up and down the room. 'Where the devil is she? She's always down to dinner on time.'

'Perhaps she's not hungry,' remarked Lady Morgan shortly, and looking at his aunt's affronted features, Oliver heaved a sigh.

'Look,' he said, halting by her chair, 'I knew Alix wasn't the librarian she claimed to be.'

'What?' Lady Morgan was astounded. 'But how?'

Oliver shrugged. 'Her lack of interest in the books in the library, to begin with. There are some valuable first editions there, books a librarian would recognise instantly. Alix never even gave them a second glance.'

'And you let her stay?' deplored his aunt.

'Yes.' Oliver was abrupt.

'Might one ask why?'

Oliver raked a hand through his hair. 'In the beginning, she intrigued me. Then, when I guessed what might be happening, I wanted to change her opinion of me.' He paused. 'I didn't plan what came after.'

'You became attracted to her?'

Oliver's lips twisted. 'That's a mild way of putting it.'

Lady Morgan got up from her chair, twisting her handkerchief between her fingers. 'So you're letting her stay?'

He nodded. 'If she will.'

Lady Morgan chewed anxiously at her lower lip. 'I see.'

'Why?' Oliver frowned suddenly, struck by his aunt's apparent distress. 'What is it?' He hesitated. 'What have you been saying to her?'

'Me?' Lady Morgan turned innocent eyes in his direction. 'What could I have been saying to her?'

'You could have told her about—about Melissa.' He stared at her intently, noticing the way her teeth dug deeper into her lip. 'You did, didn't you? You told Alix about Melissa. Why? When?'

Lady Morgan sighed, sinking down into her chair again. 'I—well, this afternoon, if you must know.'

'When you had *tea*?' Oliver scowled.

'Yes.'

He uttered an oath. 'Why did you consider it your duty to tell Alix a thing like that? I intended to tell her myself.'

His aunt moved her shoulders in a dismissing gesture. 'I felt she ought to know.'

'Really?' He looked sceptical. 'Was that all you told her?'

'What else is there?'

'There's Uncle Andrew's will, isn't there?' he reminded her dryly. 'But you wouldn't mention that, would you?'

Lady Morgan's breathing was quick and shallow. 'Oliver, what I told that girl was said with the best of intentions—'

'For whom? For me? For you? Or for Melissa?'

'Oliver, Melissa is my granddaughter!' she protested imploringly.

'I know that. Who better?' He heaved a deep sigh. 'Grizelda, I've told you, Melissa's future is secure.'

His aunt blew her nose once more. 'Do you—do you intend to marry Alix?'

'If she'll have me.'

'Oh, she'll have you, all right,' muttered Lady Morgan bitterly. 'I knew she would. That was why—'

She broke off, but not before Oliver had heard those few damning words. 'That was why—what?' he demanded. 'Grizelda, what else did you tell her? What else did you say?'

His aunt looked up at him appealingly. 'Oliver, you're a virile man. There may be children—'

'I hope so,' he confirmed grimly.

'And—and then Melissa—'

'Oh, for God's sake!' he swore violently. 'Money isn't everything, Grizelda, although you and your family have made it seem so. Melissa will be far happier growing up with other children than in some rarefied adult atmosphere!'

'Joanne never wanted her, Oliver. When you did, I—I was so happy.'

'Oh, Grizelda! How can I convince you? My feelings for Alix don't affect my love for Melissa!'

'If only Joanne could have had other children. . .'

'Grizelda, Joanne and I were washed up long before Melly was born. I guess I was too dedicated to my work. Joanne needed constant—companionship.'

'But if you'd had children!'

'Joanne didn't want children to begin with, and by the time she'd decided it wouldn't be a bad idea, I'd changed my mind. I didn't think it was fair to bring kids into our kind of relationship.'

'And yet Suomo—'

'Grizelda, that trip to Japan was supposed to be a kind of trial period. We were going to try to make the marriage work. As you know, it didn't turn out like that.'

His aunt looked down at her hands. 'And yet—and yet Joanne told me that—that Melissa could have been your child.'

Oliver uttered a bitter laugh. 'Yes, I guess she could, at that,' he agreed dryly. 'Except that she's not—is she?'

Lady Morgan shook her head. 'And you never knew. . .'

'How could I? I went to the States later that year. By the time I got back it was all over, wasn't it?'

'Joanne would have aborted the child if she could.'

'I don't doubt it.'

Lady Morgan bit her lip. 'I—I wouldn't let her.'

'You!' Now it was Oliver's turn to look stunned. 'But I thought—she said—'

'—that the doctors wouldn't allow it. I know. But that wasn't true, Oliver. When she told me that she—that you and she had—well, I persuaded her that it might be your child!'

'My God!' Oliver closed his eyes for a moment, and then opened them again. 'My God, so that's why. . .'

'Why I feel so responsible for Melissa? Yes. I feel as though I brought her into the world. The fact that she was lame as well seemed like the final humiliation to Joanne.'

'It would!' Oliver shook his head. 'Grizelda, how could you live with this and not tell me?'

'I wouldn't have if—if—'

'—if I wasn't in love with someone else?'

'Yes.'

He sighed. 'Well, you've told me now, and as it happens, it makes not the slightest bit of difference.'

'What do you mean?'

'If Alix could care about me, believing that Melissa was my child, surely the fact that she's not can only strengthen our relationship.'

Lady Morgan gave a defeated sigh. 'Then you'd better tell her, hadn't you?'

Oliver gave her a crooked smile. 'And sort out another of the problems you created?' he asked. 'Didn't your experience with Joanne teach you anything?'

'Apparently not,' his aunt replied quietly. 'I think I'll go to my room. Mrs Brandon can bring me up a tray—'

'No!' declared her nephew definitely. 'No, Grizelda, you can stay here and apologise to Alix.'

'But, Oliver. . .'

'I insist,' he said, and with a grim smile, he left her.

He mounted the stairs two at a time, and strode along the corridor to Alix's apartments. He was impatient to see her again, and he could feel the stirring excitement of his body as he contemplated making love to her later.

He knocked sharply at her door, and waited for her to answer. When she didn't, he knocked again, accompanying the action by calling her name, and turning the handle of the door when again she did not answer.

The room beyond was in darkness, and the lack of light puzzled him. Surely she couldn't be in bed, and if she was, he was still determined to speak to her. He turned the switch and lamps flooded the room with light. There was no indication of her occupation here, but this was only a sitting room after all, and after a moment's hesitation, he went through it to the bedroom beyond.

The lamps beside the bed illuminated its lack of occupation, but Oliver's eyes alighted on her suitcases with sudden apprehension. Another look about him convinced him that she was no longer in the apartments, and with an angry exclamation he strode back through the lounge and out on to the landing.

The first person he saw was Makoto, hovering nervously at the head of the stairs. She looked questioningly at him as he brushed past her to descend, and on impulse, he said: 'Have you seen Mrs Thornton?'

'Thornton *san* gone,' she stated, with a bow.

Oliver, who had been continuing on his way, expecting a negative answer, turned and came striding back to her. 'What did you say?' he demanded.

Makoto's enigmatism had never annoyed him as much as it did at that moment. 'Thornton *san* gone, Morgan *san*,' she repeated politely, and Oliver clenched his fists.

'Yes, yes, I heard you. What do you mean, she's gone?'

Makoto bowed again. 'Makoto see Thornton *san* going away this evening,' she intoned. 'Thornton *san* go in Landrover with man and woman.'

'Faulkner and his assistant?' demanded Oliver angrily. 'She didn't go with them, Makoto!' he snapped impatiently. 'Giles took them back to Newcastle, to catch the train.' He shook his head. 'She didn't go with them.'

'Oh, yes, Morgan, *san*,' insisted Makoto primly. 'Makoto go outside and see Thornton *san* hiding in the back of Landrover.'

'*What*?' Oliver couldn't believe it. 'You mean when Giles brought the Landrover and the others were getting in front—'

'—Thornton *san* get in back,' agreed Makoto demurely. 'Thornton *san* unhappy here. She want to leave. Makoto know.'

'How do you know?'

'My Missy say so. My Missy say Thornton *san* want to go back to London.'

'Oh, God!'

With an oath, Oliver descended the stairs again, crossing the hall to the dining room with scarcely concealed fury. His aunt saw his expression and trembled before it.

'Wh—what is it, Oliver?' she stammered. 'What's wrong?'

'Alix has gone!' declared Oliver grimly. 'She hid in the back of the Landrover that took Faulkner and the other girl to Newcastle. She's probably on her way to London by now.'

'Oh, Oliver!' Not for the first time his aunt felt a terrible sense of responsibility for what she had done. 'Oliver—I'm sorry.'

'Yes, so am I.'

Oliver flung himself into his chair, and when Mrs Brandon appeared to ask whether they were ready for dinner, he refused any food. Lady Morgan didn't feel like eating either, and the housekeeper had to suppress her disappointment as she went back to the kitchen. Her roast beef was going to be spoiled, but even she sensed that something more serious had occurred.

'My guess is it's that Mrs Thornton,' she told her daughter sagely. 'Always said Mr Morgan had a fondness for her. And what with her husband arriving and all, there was bound to be trouble.'

'He wasn't her husband,' muttered Myra reluctantly. 'I heard her telling Morgan. Should have seen Makoto's face when I told her!'

In the dining room, Oliver dragged himself up out of his chair with difficulty, and his aunt looked at him anxiously. 'Where are you going?'

'For a walk,' he replied coldly, 'if you've no objections.'

Lady Morgan bit her lip. 'It's snowing,' she said uneasily. 'Seth's just been in to tell me. He says it will be inches deep by the morning.'

'Is that intended as a warning?' asked Oliver bitterly.

'What do you mean?'

'I mean I intend to go to London tomorrow, whatever the weather,' he told her harshly, and slammed out of the room.

Alix was cold. She had shouted until she was hoarse, and hammered on the doors of the garage until her hands were numb, but nobody seemed to hear her. Eventually she had to return to the comparative warmth of the car, huddling in a corner at the back, grateful that at least whoever had put the car away had not locked it. But now even the car was chilled and cheerless, and without even a blanket to cover her, Alix began to shiver with the frightening realisation that she might well be there till morning.

She had given up wondering what Oliver might think about her disappearance. After all, she had planned to run away, she had packed her suitcases. Anyone seeing them would assume she had gone, and who could blame them? If it had been Giles who had driven Willie and Linsey to their destination, the gates of the Hall were unattended, and Oliver might easily think she had slipped away meanwhile. What he would say when her whereabouts were discovered was another matter, and one which she hadn't the stomach to face right now.

Some time later, she observed a curious lightening of the darkness that filtered between the cracks of the garage doors, and kneeling on the seat of the car she saw the flakes of snow being drifted under the doors by the wind that whistled eerily through the nearby trees. It was snowing, she thought despairingly, and in spite of the fact that she knew the garages were near the stables and therefore surely she would be able to attract the stable boy's attention in the morning when he came to feed the horses, she couldn't help a sense of panic that the car might not be used for days.

Then, even as she knelt there, her chin resting on her icy hands, a sudden thud hit the doors, making the head ring with the metallic echo they made. Shock kept her motionless for a moment, and it was only when she heard the dogs barking that she realised the wolfhounds had sensed her presence.

Not caring that they might be unfriendly, she scrambled quickly out of the car and ran to the doors again, shouting and banging until the animals outside went nearly wild with excitement. If only she could make sufficient noise, she might attract someone's attention, she thought desperately, although the trees and the falling blanket of snow would provide a soundproofing barrier.

Then, when her strength was giving out, and she was on the point of dropping to her knees with exhaustion, she heard a man's voice, calling the dogs. And not just any voice—Oliver's voice!

Trembling, she summoned up enough energy to call his name, but her voice was harsh after so much shouting, and had no penetration. She sank against the doors, sobbing her frustration, and fell forward into a mound of snow as Oliver wrenched them open.

'My God! *Alix*!' he exclaimed, pushing the dogs away and dropping on to his knees beside her. 'Oh, Alix! Alix! I thought you'd gone!'

She looked up at him helplessly, her heart in her eyes, and with a muffled groan he hauled her into his arms, burying his face in the hollow of her neck.

For several seconds they remained like that, and then Oliver rose abruptly to his feet, lifting her with him into his arms, unwilling to let her go even for a moment. The falling snow was covering them in a cloak of white, and without waiting for explanations, Oliver strode with her back to the house.

In the hall, Lady Morgan came hurrying to meet them, staring in amazement at the girl in her nephew's arms. 'Alix!' she exclaimed. 'But, Oliver, you said—'

'Not now, Grizelda!' he told her abruptly. 'Alix is frozen. She needs a hot bath and something warm to drink—preferably brandy. Can you see to that?'

His aunt nodded, and Alix, feeling obliged to say something, croaked: 'I—I got locked in the garage, Lady Morgan. I'm sorry if I've been a nuisance.'

Lady Morgan shook her head helplessly. Then, seeing her nephew's impatience, she nodded and hurried away towards the kitchen. Oliver, ignoring Alix's plea to be put down, continued on his way up the stairs, turning left along the landing, taking her to his rooms and not her own. He eventually set her on her feet in his sitting room, and Alix swayed dazedly as the warmth flooded back into her chilled limbs.

Oliver left her to go into his bathroom, and moments later she heard the sound of water gushing into the bath. He came back to her, gesturing behind him.

'Can you undress yourself?' he demanded, his voice full of some suppressed emotion, and she nodded quickly.

'I—thank you for—for finding me,' she began, but he silenced her with a look.

'The dogs found you,' he said. 'Get into the bath!' and turning, he strode out of the room, leaving her alone in his suite.

Alix looked after him uncertainly. What now?

What did he mean by that embrace in the snow? Where had he thought she had gone? And why had he brought her here, to his rooms? She didn't think she could face another scene, not now, and the weakness in her bones that she felt every time she was near him might not sustain her determination to refuse what he might ask of her.

She was shivering uncontrollably, and deciding that no good could come of developing pneumonia, she took off her coat and scarf and went into the bathroom. The water was still running, filling the bath with some pine-scented fragrance, and she quickly turned off the taps before taking off the rest of her clothes.

Never had water felt so good, lapping all about her like a soothing balm. Oliver's soap was pine-scented, too, and as she smoothed it over her skin, she couldn't help the intoxicating realisation that it had soaped Oliver's skin, too.

'Have you nearly finished?'

Oliver's voice made her reach blindly for the sponge, holding it defensively to her breasts. But it was a futile effort, and he took no notice of her embarrassment as he came to stand beside the bath, looking down at her with undeniable enjoyment.

'Please. . .' she exclaimed, her face flushing to match the rest of her. 'Oliver—go away!'

'Why?' He came down on his haunches beside her, lean and disturbing in his tight-fitting jeans and navy shirt. 'Shall I join you?'

Alix's pulses raced at his nearness. 'Oh, Oliver,' she breathed huskily, and putting out his hand he cupped the back of her neck, tipping her face up to his.

'I love you,' he told her unsteadily, and covered her parting lips with his.

She felt his free hand tug the sponge away from her unresisting fingers before moulding the swelling fullness of her breasts. Then, with an exclamation, he lifted her bodily out of the bath and into his arms, uncaring that she was soaking him to the skin.

'Do you love me?' he urged, reaching for a towel and wrapping it round them both, and his answer was in the way she wound her arms about his neck and pressed herself against him. 'So why did you try to run away?' he demanded savagely.

Alix trembled and pulled herself out of his arms, noticing inconsequently that his shirt and pants reflected the outline of her wet body. Then she wrapped the towel about herself, and began to dry herself self-consciously.

'Well?' he probed, unbuttoning his shirt. 'Are you going to tell me?'

'Oliver. . .' She pressed her lips together helplessly. 'I'm sorry about—about deceiving you.'

'So you should be. But that doesn't explain why you ran away.'

'Doesn't it?' She sighed. 'But surely—you said yourself you could—you could break every bone in my body.'

'For pretending you were married, yes, I could.'

'For pretending I was married?' Alix stared at him uncomprehendingly.

'Yes. Do you realise I nearly—' He broke off

abruptly, pulling his shirt off his shoulders to reveal the tanned muscular hardness of his chest. 'Alix, I thought you were experienced!'

She frowned. 'That makes a difference?'

His lips twisted. 'Slightly.'

'You mean—to your feelings?'

'No!' he snapped impatiently. 'To the way I'd have made love to you.'

'Oh!' She coloured again, and he swore.

'Alix, have you ever slept with a man?'

'No!'

'All right. So take my word, there is a difference.'

She bent her head. 'I've never—I've never let any man touch me as—as you've touched me.'

He took a step towards her, and then abruptly turned away, as if he couldn't trust himself. 'Go on!' he muttered, and she noticed the thickening in his tone.

'Well. . .' She licked her lips. 'I thought—with Willie coming here. . .'

'Faulkner?'

'Yes. I thought—I thought you'd want me to go.'

'Is that all?' He glanced at her over his shoulder.

Alix tucked the ends of the towel toga-wise about her. 'Not—not entirely,' she admitted.

'What else?'

He walked through to his bedroom, unbuttoning his wet pants as he went, and she hovered nervously in the bathroom, waiting for him to come back.

'Well?' He appeared in the doorway again, pulling on a silk dressing robe, and her mouth felt dry as she realised he was as naked as she was beneath the thin material.

'Your—your mother-in-law. . .' She used the term deliberately. 'She told me about—about Melissa.'

'So? That makes a difference?'

'I think so.'

'What do you mean?'

His brows descended grimly, and she hastened on: 'I—I do love you, Oliver, you know that, but—but I can't just—*live* with you. I—well, I'd want your children, and—and not illegitimately.'

'What in hell are you talking about?' he demanded violently, grasping her shoulders and jerking her towards him. 'What do you mean? You can't just—live—with me? Have I asked you to?'

Alix trembled. 'I—why, no, but I thought—'

'Oh, Alix!' He was not immune to the agony in her face, and hauling her towards him he buried his face in the silken softness of her hair, moulding her slender body against his. 'Alix, you fool, I want to marry you! Whoever gave you the idea I wanted anything else?'

Alix pulled her head back to stare at him. 'But you can't. Oliver, you can't. I won't let you.'

He shook his head uncomprehendingly. 'You won't let me—what?'

'Oliver, you can't deprive Melissa—'

'Who's depriving Melissa of anything?' he demanded, half angrily. 'In God's name, Alix, I'm a man. I love Melissa, but I *need* you!'

She moved her head helplessly from side to side. 'I—I can't let you do it,' she breathed. 'Oh, God—

all right, I'll live with you. But if I get pregnant—'

'Which you will,' he told her huskily, and she gave him a despairing look. 'Alix,' he added gently, 'so long as you love me, nothing can stop me from marrying you. Don't you know that?'

'But what about Melissa?' she protested.

'Melissa already knows how I feel,' he stated grimly. 'I cleared that little matter up some time ago.'

'But the money. . .'

'What money?'

She swallowed convulsively, but she had to go on. 'Your—your uncle's will—he didn't intend for you to marry again, did he?'

'What are you talking about?' Oliver took a backward step to gaze at her in a puzzled fashion. Then an idea seemed to occur to him. 'Alix, what exactly did Grizelda tell you?'

She put up a confused hand to her head. 'About—about how your uncle left all his money to Joanne so long as you didn't divorce her.'

'*What?*' He was incredulous.

'And how it's only yours if—if you don't marry again.'

'What utter rubbish!' Oliver was half amused, half furious. 'My God! No wonder she wanted to disappear before you came on the scene.'

'Who?'

'Grizelda. Who else?' He sighed, linking his arms loosely around her. 'Alix, my darling, Uncle Andrew left his fortune to me—not to Joanne, I'm sorry to say. I didn't want it, but he didn't ask my permission. That was why, after he was dead, we stayed together.

Because, God help me, I felt responsible for her.'

'But—' Alix tried to take this in, but only one thing was burning itself into her consciousness—if Joanne's father had left his money to Oliver, Oliver had had no reason to dispose of his wife to get his hands on it, as people had suggested.

'Alix,' he was speaking again, more gently now, 'I know what Grizelda was trying to do. You see, because of her, Joanne didn't have the child aborted. It could have been mine, you see, and Grizelda was desperate for us to stay together.'

'Oh, Oliver!' Alix touched his cheek, and he pulled her more closely against him so that she could feel all the hardening angles of his body.

'Alix,' he groaned softly, 'I have to tell you this, but right now there are other things I want to do.'

Her lips parted tremulously. 'Go on.'

'You make it very difficult,' he uttered, but resting his forehead against her, he continued: 'All right. Joanne had a daughter. Melissa's father, by the way, died in a plane crash before she was born.' Alix nodded, and he went on, 'So—Joanne's daughter was kept a secret until Joanne decided to let me know. Contrary to her expectations, I wanted to see the child, and the rest you can guess. I wanted her brought back to England. Joanne didn't. The outcome was a row from which Joanne emerged in a flaming temper, and—she had the crash.'

'So that was why. . .'

'. . .why she drove so recklessly? I'm afraid so. I didn't want it to happen, but Melissa deserved better than to be hidden away in Japan. She is a Morgan, after all.'

'But why did Lady Morgan. . .'

'. . .pretend things were different? Well, she knew I'd agreed to adopt Melissa. I guessed she thought if I fell in love with someone else and had children of my own, that might put Melissa's future in jeopardy.'

'Oh, Oliver!'

'Oh, Oliver!' he mimicked her gently. 'And how do you think I felt when I discovered you'd disappeared without even giving me a chance to tell you how I felt?'

'But Willie—'

'Faulkner was never a threat.'

'I worked for him,' she insisted.

'Did you? How much copy did you send him?'

'I—none.'

Oliver half smiled. 'You got under my skin from the first day you came here. I tried to tell myself I was a fool, that you were married even if you were separated from your husband, but nothing worked. So I tried to keep away from you. And you know what happened.'

Her lips quivered. 'But Melissa—'

'Yes, Melissa. She didn't like it much at first, but after I had a talk with her, I think she began to understand the situation.' He paused. 'Now tell me how you got into the garage.'

'Can't you guess?' she whispered, burying her face in the parting between the lapels of his gown.

'You tried to leave with Faulkner and his assistant?'

'Hmm.' She shivered with the memory of it, and his arms tightened.

'So you were in the car when I put it away in the garage.'

'*You* put it away?' she exclaimed. 'Yes, I was in the boot.'

He shook his head. 'Who did you think it was? Giles took our unwelcome visitors to Newcastle.'

'But what did Willie say? Didn't he want to speak to me?'

'Oh, yes. But I told him you were my fiancée, and that was why you hadn't anything to say to him.'

'But he saw Melissa!'

'I know that. And he'll probably tell the world that she's my daughter. I've told him if he does, I'll sue.'

'Oh, Oliver, can you?'

'Of course. I have proof that she's not, and unless Faulkner does a lot more ferreting, he'll never find out she's really Joanne's child.'

'I—I can hardly believe it's over,' she breathed, 'that this is actually happening.'

'Can't you?' he inquired mockingly, and feeling the penetrating hardness of his body Alix coloured anew.

'Well—perhaps,' she conceded, and for a few moments he was intent on proving to her that his hunger for her was very real.

Then he said softly: 'Do you realise if it hadn't been for the dogs, you could have spent the night in the garage? You could have died of exposure!'

'You really thought I'd gone, then?' she asked.

'Makoto told me she had seen you climbing into the back of the Landrover.'

'What?'

He nodded grimly. 'What she actually saw was you climbing into the back of the car, but she wanted to punish you for telling tales on her. She never thought—or so she says—that there was any danger of you freezing to death!'

'Oh, Oliver!' Alix stared at him.

'I've just had a few well chosen words with that lady, and I've told her she'll be on her way back to Hokkaido if she attempts to hurt you again.'

'Poor Makoto.' Alix had it in her heart to feel sorry for the little Japanese woman now. 'What about—what about your aunt?'

Oliver bent his head to caress her shoulder with his lips. 'Grizelda knows exactly how I feel. Now. . .' Determinedly he drew away from her, and indicated a tray on the table beside the bed. 'Some brandy, I think. Are you hungry?'

Watching him go and pour her drink, Alix thought she had never felt so ecstatically happy. With a little exclamation she went after him, and when he turned she was close beside him.

'I love you, Oliver,' she whispered softly, and he was not proof against her overwhelming attraction.

'The brandy. . .' he murmured as she reached up to kiss him, but she shook her head.

'Later,' she said, winding her arms about him, unfastening the cord of his robe, wanting to feel his skin against hers. As he pressed her close against him she thought that tonight Myra might well be right. Her bed would not be slept in.